D1246361

PARSE GALAXY BOOK 2

BOUNTY WAR

KATE SHEERAN SWED

JOIN THE LIST!

Join my newsletter list to get "Highly Irregular," an exclusive *Parse Galaxy* story! You'll also get access to my VIP library, which has lots of other free stuff to read.

Sign up here: https://katesheeranswed.com/highly-irregular/

CHAPTER 1

SLOANE WASN'T sure which of Scope's characteristics offended her the most: the boxlike shape that appeared to be the template for every building she passed, or the fact that it was all so uniformly *beige*. A sandcastle might manage to be beige without boring her to tears, but this place looked like the work of an unimaginative bureaucrat on a very hard deadline.

The whole place gave off a general impression of over-cooked oatmeal. If it wasn't for the occasional flash of a colorful sticker that the passing hov-tile riders had fixed to their boards, Sloane was sure her eyes would be revolting out of sheer boredom. Even the sky gave off a dusky yellow glow, as if it had simply given up trying.

She couldn't help wondering if those hov-tilers ever got pulled over for decorating with color. Purple would be a five-token offense. Red? Fifty tokens.

"Nothing unsavory could ever happen in a place like this," she said.

Brighton shot her a sideways glance. This was his first job as her new security officer, and he didn't seem at all certain he wanted to keep the job. "Don't sound so disappointed."

She really shouldn't be, especially with her arm still bound in a sling after nearly being torn off a few days ago. She'd gone ping-ponging through *Moneymaker*'s engine room during a battle, and though the arm had come in handy in preventing her from falling to her death, it was now fractured in several places. Not even the nano-healers could do much to speed up her recovery. They kept the pain at a minimum, though.

If she managed to stay out of trouble, it might even have a chance to heal fully.

Trouble did have an uncanny way of finding her, however. No matter what she did.

"I just thought someone as mysterious as this Ivy person would want to meet us in a dark club with lots of corner booths," she said. "Or a back alley, or maybe a deserted park. With lots of hanging vines."

"Are you done?"

"No. A rooftop might also be a good—"

"Too bad," Brighton interrupted, "because we're here."

Brighton held up his fliptab, where the location pin pulsed a bright green to indicate that they'd reached the coordinates Ivy had sent.

Lots of people offered Sloane jobs these days, but Ivy stood out. Because of her mysteriousness, obviously, and the fact that she looked like a vid star. But mostly it was because she'd claimed to know the whereabouts of the data key Uncle Vin had stolen before he'd disappeared. Sloane had stolen it *for* him, actually, on a job they'd done well before his disappearance. Which was why she'd dismissed the idea that the key could be linked to whatever had happened to him.

But then Ivy had shown up, offering her the location of the data key in exchange for her help, and Sloane had been rethinking the connection ever since. At least when she hadn't been busy dodging angry cartel members and defaulting on bounty deliveries.

Sloane glanced around, noticing for the first time that Brighton had led them down a narrow side street. It was *almost* narrow enough to count as an alley. The buildings here looked like squashed versions of the unimpressive tower blocks on the main street; long and wide, their suntanned siding was interrupted only by the occasional steel door.

"Warehouses?" she asked.

Brighton was staring at the door like he might see through it if he just squinted hard enough. "Seems that way."

"At least she's not waiting for us in some diner that only serves half-cooked potatoes and milk."

"I don't know what that means."

Sloane waved a hand toward the building. "Just that this is more mysterious. And you know, everything here is disturbingly...pale."

"If you have to explain a joke," he said, "then it's not funny."

"It's funny to me."

Brighton rolled his eyes and bent toward the door, listening. Sloane didn't imagine he could hear much through that thick slab of metal, and she must have been right, because a few seconds later, he touched a hand to the knob and turned it.

"It's open," he said.

"I mean, she *is* expecting us. But maybe we should knock."

Brighton ignored the suggestion and eased the door open, sticking his ear up against the crack. "Someone's fighting in there."

Had Brighton's bulk not been blocking her way, Sloane would already have knocked. Or yanked the door open to go barreling into the warehouse.

Hiring a security officer came with all kinds of benefits. Instead of barreling into trouble, she now knew she ought to try sneaking into it first.

"Maybe Ivy runs a fighting ring." She only had to bend slightly to fit her head under Brighton's arm and wedge her ear in for a closer listen. "Let's go in. Quietly."

Brighton craned his neck to look down at her from the other side of his arm. "Or we could leave and take a Federation-approved job."

"I doubt that's an option, since I basically spit in their faces when I decided not to turn you in."

"Thanks for that, by the way," Brighton said.

"Don't mention it."

She'd pay for the decision to hire Brighton, no doubt. The Federation would never let an insult like that slide. Bad for business. But she couldn't bring herself to turn Brighton in, not after he'd helped her defeat the Fox Clan and their crazy-huge spaceship that was as big as some moons.

Of course, he'd also tried to steal one of her pods. But it was in the past. Less than a week in the past, but still. The past.

Brighton rubbed his nose with his free hand. "I still think we could ditch this job and find something... gentler."

Sloane shook her head, her hair brushing the underside of his arm. In spite of his dangerous reputation and brutish size, Brighton was turning out to have more in common with a kitten than anything else. A very nervous kitten.

Ivy's job was the first real lead she had, the first true chance of finding Uncle Vin. And she *had* to find him.

"Leaving is not an option," Sloane said.

She started to slip under Brighton's arm, but he moved to block her path, planting a scowl on his face. "At least let me go first."

Sloane paused. "Okay, but only because that's what I pay you for."

She let Brighton take the first two steps before she slipped in after him, closing the door quietly behind her. The place smelled like sawdust and wet concrete, and a thin layer of water covered the floor underfoot like an oil slick. It took a solid effort to silence her footfalls as she moved across it.

For such a big man, Brighton was surprisingly light on his feet. He seemed to have no trouble keeping quiet as he scampered—she couldn't think of a better description for the way he moved, like an ox tiptoeing through a cramped candy shop, trying not spill the sweet beans—toward a pile of crates by the wall.

Warehouses were so useful that way.

When Sloane joined him behind the crates, peering out to get a good glimpse of the scene, it was clear that they'd wasted their silent entrance. A parade might have crashed into this place without being noticed.

In the center of the space, Ivy was tied to a chair, hands secured behind her back, while a pair of thugs with intense body mods loomed over her. Her bindings looked uncomfortably tight, her shoulders rounded back slightly, and though Sloane couldn't quite see her feet, her legs were tucked close enough to suggest that they were bound, too.

One of the thugs had a short crop of bleached blonde hair and four thick mechanical limbs that reached out of her spine to form a kind of gate between Ivy and the exit. Sloane didn't know how the woman could even stand with those tentacle-arms undulating around like that. A reinforced skeleton, maybe? At first, it hardly seemed necessary for her to block the exit, with Ivy restrained as she was.

Until the second thug—he had on orange-tinted sunglasses—attempted to swing a punch at Ivy's face. Judging by the click-and-squeal motor sounds that accompanied the movement, he'd been modded with extra strength. It sounded like he could use a good dose of oil, though Sloane had no idea how that worked.

"Is this the kind of excitement you pictured?" Brighton asked.

Sloane licked her lips. "Bit too far, actually."

As Sloane watched, trying to figure out the best way to barge into this situation without getting Ivy killed—or herself, for that matter—Ivy twisted and threw her body to the floor, using the legs of the chair to hit Sunglasses in the face. She'd managed to free her hands, and she did a kind of cartwheel until she was back upright, chair and all.

Maybe Ivy didn't need their help, after all.

"The modded ones are bounty hunters," Brighton said. "I've met them before. Is this a trap?"

Still gawking at Ivy's fighting technique, Sloane shook her head slowly. "I don't think so. That's Ivy in the chair."

When Sloane had first met Ivy in the club, the woman's intricate lacework of tattoos had illuminated her dark brown skin with threads of glowing silver light. Now, they were more like the rainbow-colored designs Sloane had always associated with every Interplanetary Dweller she'd ever met. Not that she'd met many, but Oliver's tattoos had looked like this. Why had Ivy's changed?

A question for later. Now it was time to join the fight.

Ivy clearly knew some kickass fighting techniques, but Sunglasses was crawling back to his feet. The chair had left a huge red welt on across his cheek. That had to hurt.

Before Brighton could stop her, Sloane abandoned the crates, freeing her old-school laser pistol from her belt. It was one of Vin's old weapons, and it'd been stuck on 'stun' for weeks now. She couldn't get it to toggle back. Not that she wanted to go around murdering people, but sometimes a well-aimed laser slice to the thigh could come in handy.

What she wouldn't give for a hand cannon right about now. Or a set of Commander Fortune's stun cables.

But the stunner was what she had. With her uninjured arm, she aimed it at Octo Girl, but Sunglasses caught sight of her and called out a warning. Octo Girl flinched out of the way in time for the stun bounce off of one of the mechanical arms.

The shot glanced off, flickering up toward the ceiling, and Octo Girl bared her teeth as two of the tube-like arms shot toward Sloane. She ducked, pushing herself into a roll as the arms cracked into the concrete behind her.

Octo Girl raised a third tentacle, but Brighton raced in from the side and leapt up to grab the flying limb, managing to wrestle it down to the ground. "Are you positive we're joining the right side of the fight here?"

Sloane picked herself up off the floor, nodding. She didn't want to say anything about the data key, not where these bounty hunters could hear, but Ivy was her only lead.

Besides, she was inclined to assume that the people who'd tied a woman to a chair were the ones with the looser morals. Just as a general principle.

Brighton wrapped his arms around the bounty hunter's modded limb and pulled, hard enough to wrench Octo Girl off her feet. "I hope you're right."

"So do I."

Up close, Octo Girl's mods didn't look sleek; the long tube-like limbs were pocked with rusty pinpricks, and they lacked the fluid movement of professional cybernetics, jerking around with graceless punches. Not, she suspected, professionally installed.

They might have been built in a dirty Fringe-based garage, but the unpredictability of the movements made them harder to fight. Though to be fair, Sloane had never fought a *well*-installed set of tentacles, so it was hard to say if that was the norm.

Sloane lifted the gun, wishing for lasers or bullets or anything else as she fired a second time. This hit landed on Octo Girl's shoulder, but it seemed to have no effect; she didn't freeze or fall. She didn't even hiss in a breath of irritation.

Useless, useless weapon.

Using a second arm to claw at the still-hanging Brighton, Octo Girl shot a third toward Sloane, knocking her stunner right out of her hands. The damn woman was everywhere at once, and there was no way to stop her.

Sloane dove toward the stunner—the weapon might be useless, but it was the only one she had—expecting Octo Girl to lift her off her feet any second. But Brighton must have recalled the woman's attention, because no hit came.

Sloane tumbled into the center of the room, her injured arm radiating pain up to her shoulder. She ignored it, and the voice in her head that suggested she might have waited to book this meeting until after the arm was healed. Too late for pragmatism. Besides, Ivy might not *survive* this fight without her help. Dubious as it was.

Ivy was still half attached to the chair, yet she was

somehow managing to kick Sunglasses' ass. He was wary of her now, skipping away every time the woman flinched.

Ivy caught Sloane's eye. "The remote," she said, ticking her chin toward a nondescript black box in the corner. It looked like something that had fallen out of someone's pocket during the fight.

Hoping against hope that she'd chosen the right ally, Sloane changed course and bolted for the remote. It seemed impossibly far away.

The last time Sloane had met Ivy, the woman had bypassed her eye screen's security barrier to send her a direct message without permission. Either she hadn't thought to do that now, or she was somehow unable to; either way, Sunglasses had obviously heard her shout to Sloane.

He abandoned his fight against Ivy and rushed for Sloane, his souped-up strengths carrying him across the room at double her pace.

Tuning out the shouts and crashes that still echoed behind her, Sloane dove for the little black box. She caught hold of it as Sunglasses' hands closed around her ankle, and she pulled it to her chest next to her sling-bound arm, clutching it hard. It had a pair of rectangular buttons, one red, the other silver.

"The silver button!" Ivy's voice somehow cut through the noise of the fight. "Press the silver button!"

Sincerely hoping that it would not blow her into the sky, Sloane pressed the button.

With her nose in the concrete, she couldn't see what happened next. But Sunglasses' fingers relaxed around her ankle, and when Sloane wrenched away from him, he fell back. She staggered to her feet and aimed her stunner at him, but he was already curled into a ball on the floor, apparently unable to move.

Before Sloane could ask him what the hell was happening, she realized the room had fallen silent. She looked up to see Brighton standing over Octo Girl, who'd also collapsed in a heap, laid out on top of her extra limbs, as if they were too heavy to keep lifting. She looked like a beetle, turned onto its back.

Keeping her stunner at the ready, just in case, Sloane hobbled back across the space. Ivy had somehow freed herself from the chair, and she stood next to it, back straight, chin high. She had a shallow cut on her cheek and a light sheen of sweat dewing her rich brown skin. Her tattoos were once again giving off their calm, silvery glow. "Thank you," she said.

Sloane paused. "You did that," she said. "It wasn't that remote. It was you."

"I turned off their mods, yes. Too heavy to handle without power."

And they must have turned hers off before that. Though Sloane had never seen tattoo mods like that—she wasn't even sure if they *were* mods, or if they were something else. She'd always thought the Interplanetary Dwellers simply wore colorful geometric tattoos, that it was a cultural thing. Oliver had never been able to do anything fancy with them.

He'd have used them to steal stuff and betray people, but still. He'd definitely have used them.

Sloane still didn't know for sure that Ivy *was* an Interplanetary Dweller, though the way the tattoos had changed into those familiar rainbows did strengthen the theory.

Brighton whistled, long and low. "Didn't know turning off mods was a thing."

Sloane hadn't known, either—seemed like a dangerous

power to have—but she couldn't say she was sorry. She nudged a toe against Octo Girl's nearest tentacle. The woman seemed to be unconscious. "Good night, Octo Girl," she said.

Brighton frowned. "She only has four arms."

"Don't be so literal."

"I don't see what would be so difficult about calling her Quadro Girl."

"It's not—because there are no Quadropus in the galaxy, so it would make no sense."

"You didn't call her Octopus Girl, you called her Octo Girl. That implies—"

Sloane threw up her hands. "There are eight if you count her biological arms and legs. Okay?"

Brighton was still frowning, like it didn't track. As if that was the important thing right now.

"Take it up with Alex, will you?" Sloane said. "She loves to pick apart my nonsense. She'd agree with you a hundred percent."

Brighton sniffed. "The only subject I'm taking up with Alex is her inability to do dishes."

Ivy was looking back and forth between them like she was watching a zeeball match. Not the best first impression for a potential client. Then again, they had just helped her get the remote thingy that had somehow dampened *her* tech, so that had to be a point in their favor.

Sloane cleared her throat and turned her full attention to Ivy. "You said you had a job for us. Was that the interview?"

Ivy blinked, then nodded. "Not intentionally, but yes," she said. "You'd better take me to your ship."

Brighton pointed to the passed-out bounty hunters. "And what about them?"

Ivy made for the door without so much as glancing back over her shoulder. "Don't worry," she said. "Once I'm gone, they'll be fine."

Sloane wasn't so sure that was a good thing. She hesitated, then followed Ivy out of the warehouse, Brighton on her heels.

CHAPTER 2

GARETH COULDN'T IMAGINE A MORE pleasant V-Space arrangement than this one. Only a Center System like Halorin would go to the trouble of stirring a breeze through the tree branches in the park, where rolling hills extended in every direction and a pleasant glow of sunlight warmed his skin. He even imagined he could feel the light spray of the fountain whenever the wind shifted.

He wished he could imagine that the Halorin System governors had stopped talking, but alas, the V-Space didn't include a mute setting. Which was just as well, given that Gareth was meant to be contemplating each speech with solemn concern.

And there had been several hours of speeches to solemnly contemplate, with no indication of a respite on the horizon.

It was currently Wagner Penn's turn to prattle, and the man obviously took the responsibility as seriously as he took his facial hair. His mustache had grown so long that he'd combed it in with his long gray hair, which flowed over the shoulders of his red vest. He wore a long white shirt beneath it and a prim tie secured around his neck.

And since there was no asterisk above his head to indicate he'd changed his appearance for the V-Space, Gareth had to assume Penn was sitting somewhere in the physical world wearing the very same fussy outfit, down to the last gold-enameled button.

"The Fox Clan ship is still on the float at the border of the system," Penn was saying. "Who knows how much it will cost to remove the blight?"

Penn had a lot to say for a man who'd been nestled comfortably in the absurd luxury of Ve Station throughout the entire fight. He probably hadn't even heard about the incident until after it'd concluded.

Gareth pressed his hands into the small of his back, doing his best to keep his stance open. Relaxed, but attentive. "As I've said, the Fleet will deal with the detritus from the battle. Both the task and the expense. It's what we do."

Penn gave him a steely eyed stare, as if offended at an interruption—had it been one? Gareth didn't think so—but Lydia Corinth, one of the other governors, spoke up before Penn could rebuke him.

"Can we rely upon the Fleet to share the data it finds?" Lydia tapped her fingertips together, white-painted nails reflecting against the fake sunlight.

"Absolutely not," Penn said. "We'll need to spare inspectors and bear the cost of sending them up to the ship."

Gareth wanted to shake his head. Because the richest station in the galaxy really needed to hoard its tokens like that. As Penn talked—and talked and talked—Gareth imagined the man's head like an over-filled balloon that deflated with every word he said, smaller and smaller, until it disappeared straight into the man's neck.

Either he'd been spending too much time with Sloane Tarnish, or he was getting sick of unappreciative bureaucrats. Perhaps both.

Gareth held up a hand, and the governors' heads all snapped toward him. Penn left off speaking in the middle of a sentence, mouth open, as though he couldn't believe Gareth's insolence.

Gareth half suspected that the man had forgotten he was there at all.

His father had never needed to remind people that he was the stars-damned Commander of the Parse Galactic Fleet. When he'd walked into a room, people had known. They'd paid attention.

"I didn't lead the Fox Clan into Halorin," Gareth said. "I chased them here, and I stopped them before they came anywhere near the closest atmosphere. Now, *my* ships are engaged in cleaning up your system for you. If you incurred expenses during the incident, that was your choice."

Penn's mouth worked, like a fish with a sour taste on its tongue. "But—"

"If you'd like to be angry at someone," Gareth continued, "I saw the ships leave Pike System with my own eyes. Perhaps the Cosmic Trade Federation knows something about them."

It was incredible, really, how every single one of the governors dropped their gazes to their hands. Remarkable, the kind of cowardice that the Federation could inspire. A threat to their pocketbooks was more dire than a threat to their planets.

Gareth's father had been as intimidating as the Federation. Even more so, though perhaps Gareth was biased in that respect.

Lydia recovered first, running a hand through her long

blonde hair. "Yes, well, we've discussed the matter, Commander. We'd like to speak directly with the Fleet Advisory Commission."

Gareth snapped his hands back to parade rest, parking them at his tailbone. Sometimes it was the only grounding he had. "That's not how this works."

Especially since Osmond Clay had restructured the FAC overnight, somehow clearing out representatives who'd served for decades and replacing them with his own allies. Gareth didn't know how he'd done it, or even why; he only knew he hadn't been able to reach his friend Alisa—one of the former representatives—in the three days since it'd happened.

Alisa had always been his ally. Gareth didn't know what Clay might have done to silence her. Threats? Blackmail?

He refused to think it could be anything worse. If Clay had mounted an attack in Alisa's Torrent System, he'd have heard.

"Perhaps it should be *how this works*," Penn said, his tone coming dangerously close to mocking Gareth's statement. And the other governors simply nodded, like silent consenters to a suggestion that went directly against the accords.

The Fleet didn't interfere with planetary governments, and it didn't put bases on the ground outside of Cadence System unless explicitly asked to do so. It offered arbitration and protection when System conflicts threatened to turn to violence; it brought aid in response to natural disasters and criminal enterprises. With no political affiliations, the Fleet truly kept the peace in the galaxy. His father had believed in that mission, and so did Gareth.

In return, the Systems didn't interfere with Fleet operations.

Gareth tried to imagine what his father would have done, what he'd have said to these governors who stared back with such expectant expressions. Would he have walked out of the room? Threatened to deny the support that the Fleet was honor-bound to provide? Or would he have expounded on the dangers leaking out of the Adu System in a bid to convince these coddled Center-System governors through fear?

No. Dad wouldn't have needed to do any of that. One word from James Fortune and the governors would have been scrambling to help, offering their resources without so much as a peep about what it might cost.

Gareth had served as Fleet Commander for eight years, yet he sometimes felt as though he'd stepped into the role yesterday.

The governors were still awaiting a response, peering at him from under ridiculously tall hairdos and over gem-encrusted collars. Of all the Center Systems to deal with, Halorin was the worst. Gareth could almost feel his limited power draining with every beat of delay.

"We'll handle the remains of the ship, and we'll send a complete report," he said. "As we always do."

Wagner opened his mouth—it seemed to be his default expression—but before he could launch into another speech, a green light flickered on in the middle of the meeting to indicate a newcomer to the V-Space. And then Lieutenant Martin Lager materialized at Gareth's side, his Fleet insignia shining on his shoulders as though he'd polished it for the occasion.

"Excuse the interruption, sir." Lager directed the words

to Gareth, ignoring the governors. "You're needed on the bridge urgently."

Whatever salary Lager was pulling down from the Fleet at the moment, it wasn't enough. Gareth could have kissed the man. He nodded, then turned back to the governors. "If you'll excuse me."

It wasn't a clean way to leave a meeting, or even an appropriate one, but Gareth couldn't take another second of verbal tug-of-war with these people. The park fell away, and he exited into a conference room in the mid-section of *Sabre*, the frigate that flew under his command. He'd never even left the room, yet it felt like returning home. He rubbed a hand over his face, wishing he could wipe the entire meeting from his mind.

The Halorin governors wouldn't be put off for long. He'd have to deal with them eventually.

Lager stood on the other side of the room at parade rest, hands resting behind his back. Waiting for Gareth to shake off the V-Space fog.

"At ease, Lieutenant," Gareth said. "You do know you don't actually have to enter the V-Space to call me out of a meeting."

Lager relaxed, dropping his hands to his sides. "I figured it would look more official. You seemed like you could use the help."

"How long were you listening in?"

"Long enough." Lager's smile was fleeting, which told Gareth the Lieutenant had pulled him out to deal with a real situation. As awful as the Halorin governors were, Lager wouldn't interrupt without reason. Something dire enough to necessitate Gareth's presence on the bridge.

Never a dull moment. They left the conference room together, and Gareth breathed in the bustling atmosphere of the ship. He liked Halorin's V-Space park—or he would have, had it not been full of self-serving governors—but there was nothing like the energy of an active Fleet frigate.

Here, everyone had a purpose, a job. Diplomats and scientists, soldiers and researchers. It would have been purpose enough had they only existed to keep the peace. But they studied and documented Parse history. They developed new technologies. And upon occasion, they even had cause to explore new reaches of the galaxy.

It was an exciting world. Every day an adventure.

Gareth and Lager turned toward the bridge. "Better brief me now," Gareth said. "Did we find information on the Fox Clan ship? Where it came from?"

The criminal cartel had shown up to the fight with the largest ship he'd ever seen, a behemoth of a vessel that Sloane Tarnish had taken down in her typical mad fashion: by flying an escape pod through its halls to ultimately deactivate the defense shields. The Fleet had no information on where the Fox Clan had been hiding such a large ship—it hadn't left Pike with the others—or whether there might be more like it.

An unnerving thought.

"No, sir." Lager's expression was grave, the corners of his mouth tugging down with worry. "One of our corvettes has gone missing. The *Dirk*."

They stepped onto the bridge, returning a volley of salutes from soldiers who quickly returned to their work. Gareth frowned, trying to piece together Lager's words. "Missing how?"

Lager flicked his fingers over his fliptab and brought up a map of the galaxy, tapping a reflection of his screen onto the viewport. It showed Fleet ships stationed throughout the galaxy, each marked with a blinking green dot.

As Gareth looked at this map, he couldn't help thinking how scattered the Fleet looked in comparison to the size of the galaxy. He believed in their mission, believed in their work, but sometimes it felt like looking at a handful of cotton balls trying to staunch a stab wound.

There was still a heavy concentration of Fleet presence in and around Adu System, where criminal activity threatened to boil over on a daily basis. Several ships at home in Cadence, and others out on patrol in various pockets of the galaxy.

Lager pointed to an orange spot in the band of space between Halorin System, where *Sabre* was now, and Torrent System. Alisa's system. "The ship stopped transmitting its location here. They haven't responded to any attempt at communication."

"*Dirk* was patrolling the bands?" Though it was impossible to patrol every part of the galaxy, of course, the Fleet set patrols in certain parts of the bands—the stretches of space between System clusters—where mines were prevalent. They watched for pirate activity, and for bandits that might take advantage of the mines' remote locations. The fact that the Fleet could happen by at any point sometimes acted as a deterrent to violence.

Because even when pirates operating in the bands did nothing but steal, the act still amounted to violence. Water, food supplies, and oxygen—those were the commodities thieves went after in the bands. They'd strip a mine and leave it to starve and suffocate, its residents too remote for immediate assistance.

"Yes, sir."

Gareth scanned the map. "Well, we're not going to get anything from staring at the spot where they disappeared. If they're not responding, we'll have to go out there. Could be an equipment malfunction."

"Yes, sir. Should I send *Cutlass?*"

Cutlass, another Fleet frigate, was here in Halorin helping to clean up after the Fox Clan disaster. The Currents didn't run through the bands, so proximity was relevant; *Sabre* and *Cutlass* were closest to the spot where the corvette had disappeared. It would still take several days to reach the *Dirk*'s last known coordinates from here.

"No," Gareth said. "Remit orders for *Cutlass* to wrap up work on the Fox Clan ship and tow it out to Cadence through the Current. Inform the Halorin governors of the plan as well, so they'll feel included. *Sabre* will investigate the *Dirk*'s whereabouts."

Lager blinked. "You want *us* to go, sir?"

"That's what I said, Lieutenant."

Lager glanced at the map, then tapped the orders into his fliptab. "You're not needed in Halorin, sir?"

"Not as much as I'm needed there."

Lager looked up, studying him for a long moment. More than colleagues, they were friends, and Lager didn't hesitate to question his commands. A quality Gareth appreciated, in general, though he was glad Lager dropped his voice when he said, "Why do I get the feeling this is more about you wanting to run away from the bureaucrats?"

Because it is, Gareth thought. But truly, the idea of a missing Fleet corvette niggled at his ribcage like a shard of glass. It *could* be an equipment malfunction, but something about it didn't sit right. Transponder signals didn't simply vanish. And why wouldn't they have communicated a distress signal?

Lager could deliver the news with as much official unconcern as he liked, but this wasn't a routine occurrence.

It wasn't even an infrequent one. Gareth couldn't remember it ever happening before. Fleet ships didn't just disappear.

"If my soldiers are in distress, I need to be there," Gareth said. But that almost felt like calling trouble down on himself, as though he could make it happen just by saying it—was it worse to be superstitious, or to act rashly? So he added, "Likely a malfunction, as you said. We'll find them."

Lager nodded. "Yes, sir."

Gareth watched *Sabre*'s position on the map as it inched away from the bright lights of Halorin. At full-galaxy scale, the ship was no larger than a pinprick.

"So the governors wanted to speak with the FAC." Lager's voice was barely louder than a whisper, his eyes still trained on the map, but Gareth heard him well enough. He shot the Lieutenant a warning look, but Lager just raised an eyebrow.

"You heard that part, did you?" Gareth asked.

"I did. A power play, or something more?"

Gareth shook his head. He appreciated Lager's support, but he didn't have answers yet. He needed time to think. "I don't know yet. Carry on here. I'll be in the strat room."

As soon as he closed the door behind him, Gareth opened his own fliptab and initiated a call to Alisa March. The call history said he'd tried her a dozen times over the past three days, and she hadn't answered once. If she was at home in Torrent, she'd be too far away for instant communication, but she hadn't responded with a message, either.

The fliptab offered him the chance to leave a message, and Gareth schooled his face to calm so he could record yet another video. "Alisa," he said, "I genuinely hope you're well. I'm beginning to worry."

CHAPTER 3

SLOANE COULDN'T HELP FEELING that *Moneymaker*'s kitchen was starting to get a bit crowded.

With the ship hanging in orbit around Scope, Hilda had handed the controls over to the autopilot. For the sole purpose, as far as Sloane could tell, of joining Brighton in a well-practiced impersonation of a bouncer in a high-end club. Only instead of luxing it up on Ve Station, her crew members were seated in the half-circle dining booth in the kitchen, both of them glaring at Ivy with their arms crossed over their chests, eyes narrowed into identically suspicious expressions. As though Ivy was a thief they'd caught swiping petty cash, rather than a client who wanted to pay for their services.

Hilda's parakeet hopped back and forth on her shoulder, chirping, as though it fully intended to take part in the forthcoming interrogation.

Even Alex had deigned to join them. She sat in the center of the booth, her red hair knotted in a messy bun on top of her head. She stared at Ivy, too—though her gaze was more of an awe-stricken stare, her eyes round as moons as they raked over their client's tech-tattoos. The scientist looked like she was one embarrassing moment from reaching out to touch them.

As for Ivy, she sat back in the booth with one arm stretched across the seat. Somehow, she managed to look relaxed and dangerous at the same time. She was looking back and forth between *Moneymaker*'s crew members with a faint smile on her face. Hard to interpret, really. Bemused, confused, or completely freaked out; any of those would fit the bill.

Sloane wouldn't blame her if she decided to bolt. Immediately.

She also couldn't help thinking that if they took on one more crew member or passenger—and if Brighton decided to move his cot up from the corner of engineering where he'd been crashing, even though she'd offered him Vin's cabin—Sloane would need to repurpose the cargo hold into sleeping quarters. How much cargo did they really haul, anyway?

Sloane sat across from the booth in her usual spot, perched up on the kitchen counter with her legs dangling, her injured arm tied in a new sling. It was smarting pretty hard from getting jostled around in the fight, but she'd live.

She was aching to start a pot of coffee, too, but she wasn't exactly ready to explain to Ivy that it'd come from a far-distant galaxy. And she *really* didn't want to share the limited amount she had left.

When she could take everyone's silent staring and longer, Sloane cleared her throat. If Ivy wasn't going to speak first, then she had no problem unleashing the first of the many, many questions that'd been building since first meeting the woman. And that fight in the warehouse had only added more to the collection.

"Okay," Sloane began. "What did you do to those modded thugs back there? I get that it had something to do with your tattoos, but I've known Interplanetary Dwellers—"

"She knew one of them *really* well," Alex interrupted, eyes glued to Ivy's right arm, which was still draped gracefully over the back of the seat. Her fingertips were mere inches from Alex's face, and Sloane got the sudden, irreverent image of the scientist snapping her jaw to take a bite.

Even Alex had to know that would be a faux pas. She hoped.

Sloane decided to ignore the reference to her tragic backstory and the past betrayal of her now dead ex. "The Interplanetary Dwellers I've met had rainbow-colored tattoos. They weren't..." Sloane waved a hand toward Ivy, at a loss for words.

Alex said, "Illuminated with the inner magic of pure moonlight."

"Yeah," Sloane said. "That."

Ivy held her hands out flat over the table, displaying the tattoos that ran up her wrists and disappeared into her sleeves. They made Sloane think of intricate line drawings, ancient knots with endless connections and open loops. And yet they were still unlike anything she'd encountered during her brief study of art history. They had their own style of beauty.

"My inlays can hijack nearby technology," Ivy said. "Deactivate it or repurpose it."

The deactivating part, Sloane had guessed. The repurposing part was new. And more than a bit disconcerting. "Repurpose it how?"

Ivy slid out of the booth with fluid grace, stepping across the narrow aisle to join Sloane at the counter.

Brighton followed, practically falling out of his seat to intercept Ivy at Sloane's side. What did he think their new client was going to do? Sloane had no mods to hack.

Ivy ignored him and pointed a slender finger at Sloane's arm. "You have nano-healers working on your injury?"

Okay, she had a *few* temporary mods to hack. Sloane nodded. "Still going to take another ten days. It was a bad break."

After using her poor forearm-slash-elbow to prevent certain death, she'd ended up with a dislocated shoulder and multiple fractures. It'd hurt like hell. With the nano-healers, it only hurt like hell's waiting room.

"With your permission," Ivy said, "I can use the inlays to increase their power. Your arm will be healed in hours instead of days."

Brighton inserted a protective hand between Ivy and Sloane, coming dangerously close to grazing Sloane's chest. "I don't think so," he said.

He'd only been on the crew for two days—or was it three?—and he already acted like they'd known each other for years. Sloane appreciated the thought, but she wasn't his daughter, his sister, or his niece, and she didn't need his protection unless she asked for it. Which she would, on a regular basis. He *was* the security officer.

But Sloane was the captain. She might hate the word, and she might avoid speaking it out loud, but she'd play the card if she had to. Gently, she pushed his hand away. "I'll take the risk."

Brighton faced her, concern digging deep lines into his wide forehead. "We don't know anything about this. We don't know how it works, or who she is."

"But I'd like to know," Sloane said.

Alex raised a hand. "So would I."

Brighton's lines only deepened. "You'd let her jump out an airlock if it would tell you more about the magic ink."

"I would," Alex confirmed. "I definitely would."

Sloane didn't doubt it. But she held Brighton's gaze. "I take full responsibility."

After a beat, Brighton shook his head and shuffled aside, mumbling under his breath. He stayed close though, just a pace away. Sloane didn't know what he'd be able to do if Ivy decided this would be the opportune time to use the nano-healers to murder her, but she appreciated the gesture.

She had to believe that if Ivy wanted to hurt her, she'd have done it back on Scope.

Ivy touched a finger to the back of Sloane's wrist. Her skin was cool and dry, and for a breath, nothing happened. The crew had mercifully decided to shut their mouths, and there was just the vibration of the engines humming through the counter, the hitch in Alex's breath, and the soft scrape of Hilda's nails as she rubbed them unconsciously against the tabletop.

Sloane was on the verge of asking whether the inlays had been damaged, or if she should feel anything, when a river of cold washed through her so suddenly that she gasped out loud.

It felt like someone had replaced her blood with ice water, and she shuddered, wondering if she'd made the wrong choice and if Brighton would stand up at her funeral to say, 'I told her so.'

As quickly as she considered that possibility, the coldness was gone.

Breathing deeply, Sloane looked down at her arm. "It doesn't hurt anymore." She reached up, removed the sling, and checked her range of motion. "That's...it should have taken a full ten days to heal. Maybe more."

Ivy nodded and retreated back to the booth, placing her hands down flat on the table as if she wanted to keep them where Brighton could see them. "It'll still be tender for a few hours. When you wake up, it'll be good as new."

Sloane worked her arm up and down, amazed. It didn't feel tender at all. "And you used your tech to enhance the nano-healers?"

"Yes."

"How does that work?"

Ivy shook her head. "I haven't been able to discover that. It feels like...it feels like a sixth sense. I can detect technology nearby, and I can direct my inlays to respond to it."

"With your thoughts," Sloane said.

"Not exactly, but it wouldn't be completely incorrect to picture it that way."

Still wedged into the far side of the booth, Alex leaned her face closer to the table, hovering over Ivy's hand like she hoped the tattoos would give up their secrets if she just stared hard enough. Sloane would've been willing to bet that the scientist was close to salivating.

And she claimed her interests were in astrophysics and astrophysics alone. Right.

Brighton was still hovering near Sloane, and he hissed in a breath. "How can you use tech like that when you don't know how it works? It's irresponsible."

Hilda ticked her chin forward, as if she were inclined to agree.

It was touching that he was still so worried—that they both were—but Sloane felt giddy. Like she could turn a few cartwheels if all these people would clear out of her kitchen. She nodded to Brighton, and he joined Hilda back in the booth, shaking his head. If he kept doing that, he was going to get a neck ache. She couldn't afford to take on a masseuse, and there was no room to house one even if she did.

"Okay," Sloane said, doing her best to calm herself. "Cool powers. But that doesn't explain why I've never met another Interplanetary Dweller with tattoos—inlays—like yours."

Ivy turned her palms around so they were face down on the table, and Brighton twitched as though he still expected her to attack. Hilda put a placating hand to his arm, though she hardly looked less suspicious.

"People who choose to leave the Interplanetary Dwellers get their technology deactivated before they go," Ivy said. "I didn't want that to happen, so I left in the night."

Finally, some answers. Sloane was beginning to see the connections in Ivy's story, spiderweb thin lines floating together in her mind. "So now they're sending hunters after you."

"Yes. I should have realized they would."

"Fun fact!" *Moneymaker*'s shipboard artificial intelligence, BRO, broke into the conversation with its usual enthusiastic tone. She never knew when the thing would decide to pipe up with its questionable take on a conversation. "Space has no night!"

Sloane suppressed a groan, which would only make the AI start whining about not being appreciated. It wasn't, most of the time, but the whining made it much worse.

"Or," Brighton said, "does space *always* have night?"

BRO gasped. Or at least, it made a gasping sound. Sloane didn't think it had lungs, or a trachea. "Mind. Blown," it replied.

Ivy raised her eyebrows, glancing around.

"Ignore the AI," Sloane said. "It's deranged. Why did

you want to leave the Interplanetary Dwellers in the first place?"

"Rude!" BRO said.

Sloane wasn't sure if it was referring to the deranged comment, or the direct question about the Interplanetary Dwellers, but either way, she'd never exactly been known for her subtlety. She wasn't necessarily sure it was *better* to be direct, she just...didn't know any other way.

Ivy dropped her gaze to the table, and for the first time, Sloane realized how exhausted she looked. She hid it well, with her tightly woven pair of braids and her meticulously clean outfit—even after the fight, there were no tears in her shirt—but her eyes had the barest hint of pink around the edges, and her hands were trembling. Just the smallest bit, but Sloane caught it.

"I didn't want to leave." Ivy's voice, previously direct and confident, was now soft. Not uncertain, exactly, but not...not certain, either. "They were going to kick me out for developing my own technology."

Alex's eyes lit up, and Sloane could practically see the questions bubbling up in the scientist's brain. Given the chance, Alex would grill Ivy on every detail. What had she invented, and how did it work, and could Alex please, *please* play with Ivy's toys?

Alex would have to interrogate Ivy later. Sloane didn't want to derail the conversation, not when they were finally getting somewhere, so she said quickly, "Didn't the Interplanetary Dwellers develop the inlays in the first place?"

"No." Ivy's tone was emphatic. "We're caretakers of technology. Creating it is strictly prohibited."

We. Ivy still thought of herself as one of them. Something about the detail caught at Sloane's chest like a tiny, cruel hook. "But the tattoos had to come from somewhere,"

Sloane said, doing her best to keep her voice gentle. It wasn't her forte, but she didn't think she sounded confrontational, either. "Didn't the Interplanetary Dwellers create it?"

"We didn't."

"Then where did it come from?"

Ivy shrugged. "Not our concern. We're tasked with keeping this kind of advanced technology safe and functioning, to pass it over generations, until the galaxy is ready for it."

"Who tasked you with it, though?"

"Not our concern."

Sloane glanced at Hilda, who rolled her eyes toward the ceiling. Maybe she'd encountered Interplanetary Dwellers before. Sloane would have to ask her if she knew more about that philosophy of theirs. Or religion? It was hard to say.

Funny that Oliver had never mentioned it. But then, he'd wanted to leave it all behind, hadn't he?

"Not to be rude," Hilda said, "but is there a job buried in this conversation somewhere? You promised Sloane you could find Vincent's data key."

Sloane still didn't understand how Ivy even knew about the data key, let alone its whereabouts. But if she understood what Ivy was implying, Interplanetary Dwellers had a lot of technology beyond these tattoo-inlay things. They apparently knew much more than she'd ever assumed. They might have a lot of power, too.

And they might be able to locate Uncle Vin. Though that supposed they were willing to *use* this miraculous technology of theirs.

"Fun fact!" BRO chimed in. "A 'job' is an abstract concept that cannot be 'buried.'"

"It was a metaphor, BRO," Alex said.

"Another abstract concept!"

Ivy leaned her forearms on the table. "A few months ago, a man named Damian Riddle raided one of our hidden vaults. He's a known pirate, and a thief. He doesn't seem to have figured out how to use any of the technology he stole, because it hasn't surfaced anywhere. We'd have heard about it if it did."

"I'll bet," Hilda muttered. "Tech-hijacking inlays. If that ever gets out..."

Sloane shuddered. Yeah, the wrong people would wreak havoc in the galaxy with access to that kind of technology.

"That's why we're *caretakers*," Ivy snapped, losing her calm for the first time in the conversation. "We don't *want* it to get out."

"It's like Sloane said," Hilda said, matching Ivy's heat. "The tech comes from somewhere. You're telling me you've never considered that the Interplanetary Dwellers might have some hidden lab where they cook this stuff up, then lure you all into a cult to worship it?"

Ivy was shaking her head, her hands trembling against the tabletop. "You misunderstand the entire situation."

Sloane held up a hand. They could have this conversation later, preferably from opposite ends of a very large room. "So what's the job?" she asked. "What does this Damian person have to do with anything?"

"The Interplanetary Dwellers want him more than they want me." Ivy said the words like she was testing them, like she wasn't used to speaking of her own people, her own culture, from the outside. "If I bring him back, they might be willing to make a deal."

"You think they'll let you return?" Brighton asked.

Ivy blinked rapidly, wedging her bottom lip between

her teeth, and Sloane thought she saw tears collecting in the woman's eyes. They needed to let her rest, and soon. "No. No, I closed that door. But I thought they might be willing to trade Damian for the inlays. Let me keep them, and agree to stop hunting for me."

She wanted to develop her technology, to live her own life, more than she wanted to be at home with her own people. Even if it was breaking her heart. Sloane could understand that.

Hilda snorted, dismissing Ivy's plan. "That sounds like Sloane's kind of reasoning."

Sloane shrugged. "I've heard worse ideas."

"Case in point."

"I gave up my entire world for my passion," Ivy said. "I can't develop my tech as a hunted woman, and it's the best idea I've got."

Sloane tried to imagine what it would be like to care about something enough that you'd be willing to give up everything you'd ever known to pursue it, and she came up short. Given the choice, she'd hitch a U-turn back to her home planet and give up this whole adventure.

At least, that was what she'd been telling herself. When the words crossed her mind now, it felt more like a rote answer than an actual truth. If that was why she really felt, why hadn't she returned her father's calls? He might be disapproving, but he also had the power to help. Make some calls, pull some strings, and end this misadventure once and for all.

If only she could trust him to use his power to search for his ne'er-do-well brother.

For now, Ivy must have a job for them, and the reward would be a lead on Uncle Vin's whereabouts. The first lead she'd had since he'd disappeared.

"So you want us to catch Damian for you," Sloane said.

Ivy nodded. "You've picked up a certain amount of... notoriety, over the last few months. And Damian, he's slippery. I thought you might be the one to find him."

Ivy must not have been paying attention to *how* Sloane had gained that notoriety, but Sloane wouldn't be the one to enlighten her. She slid off the counter and brushed her hands together, reveling in the complete absence of pain. Even the nano-healers had only been able to do so much to help that break. Now, she felt like she could do at least three pushups without falling over. And that was one more pushup than her previous record.

"I'll start in Vin's cabin," Sloane said. "See what I can find on Riddle. Ivy, you can stay in our former security officer's room. Hilda will show you the way."

As she headed for the spiral staircase that led down to the crew cabins, though, Hilda practically shoved Brighton out of the booth to intercept her. She caught hold of Sloane's elbow, keeping her voice low. "It sounds like you might get further looking for this Damian Riddle guy if you checked Oliver's room. Ivy could stay in Vin's."

Sloane had zero desire to go poking through her dead ex's things. She'd prefer to forget that he had ever existed in the first place. "What, just because he was an Interplanetary Dweller? You heard what Ivy said. He didn't have access to the tech."

"No. Because his console is the one with the black-market contacts and under-feed access. His stuff is much more recent, too."

And probably as unreliable as he'd been. The idea of going into his room only got harder as time passed, not easier. It wasn't an option. "Vin's got plenty of information to work with. Get Ivy settled. I'll check in with you later."

CHAPTER 4

SABRE'S INSTRUMENTS detected the wreck long before it came into view, giving Gareth several hours to prepare himself, yet the sight of it still caught in his throat. A ragged crescent of scorched hull, it simply hung there in the darkness, as if someone had dropped it into a tub of cryo gel before activating deep freeze.

Wrecks out in the vacuum were rarely still. Not without interference, and even then, it was difficult to completely rid them of motion. They tended to look more like broken mobiles, turning silently in the black. Eerie, in their way, but right. Expected.

This wreck just seemed *wrong*.

"It looks old," Gareth said, afraid that there was too much hope leaking into his tone. Or too much fear.

It couldn't be the *Dirk*. It couldn't be.

But there was no way to tell. Not by sight. The thing was a twisted hunk of scrap, unrecognizable. Gareth was familiar with a good number of the commonly used ships in the galaxy, and he couldn't even begin to make a guess on the type. It might've been a freighter or a passenger shuttle. It might've been a Fleet star corvette.

"It's not the *Dirk*." Captain Reynolds said after a moment, sounding about as relieved to say it as Gareth was to hear it. His head was bent over his instruments as he scanned the preliminary data, his square-framed glasses sliding almost the full length of his nose. "Scanners picked up the last few digits of the serial. It's a water hauler."

Gareth gripped the rail, unable to wrench his gaze from the wreck. Civilians. The only relief was that he hadn't known its crew. Grief clawed at his throat, and he swallowed it back. "Any idea where they'd have been headed?"

"There's an asteroid mine a few hours out," Lager said. He was standing beside Gareth, head buried in his fliptab maps. Gareth could practically see plans running through the man's mind, strategies. "HTR-79. Probably their intended destination."

If this wreck was old, had the asteroid miners been dealing with low supplies? Did they know it was missing, or were they trying to arrange another shipment?

As soon as *Sabre* had finished up here, they'd need to head out to the mines. See if the people there needed any assistance.

"The wreck was recent." Reynolds was flipping through his own data like he couldn't quite believe it himself, and Lieutenant Stills actually got up from her communication console to study the data over his shoulder.

After a moment, she nodded, confirming Reynolds' report. "That metal is still hot."

Gareth glanced at Lager, whose eyes were narrowed in concentration. "But it's so still," he said. "How can it be so *still*, unless someone intervened?"

Usually *they* were the ones who intervened. "Perhaps

the *Dirk* was here ahead of us," Gareth said, but the words rang hollow before he'd even finished the sentence. The captain would have reported the wreck.

No one said it. No one needed to.

"There's an anomalous energy reading coming from the wreck," Reynolds said, eyes still focused on the data, Stills reading it along with him. "Not enough data yet to tell what it is."

"We'll need to send a team in for analysis." Gareth's voice sounded hollow to his own ears, distant. This was a necessary part of the job, but one he hated. He supposed a man who relished it would be ill-suited for leadership—it was a line he'd heard his mother repeat, from time to time—but the sentiment was of little comfort when he faced moments like these.

Who could have done a thing like this? Pirates and thieves scuttled around the galaxy like cockroaches, it was true, but they tended to keep their activities to the Fringe Systems. It was one of the reasons he'd been fighting so hard to keep control in Adu, to prevent them from gaining a strong foothold in a Middle System.

But the bands could be dangerous, too. He was looking at the evidence of that.

Still, he couldn't help viewing it as a personal failure. If he'd been here, he could have saved this crew.

"Sir," Lager said, interrupting his dark thoughts, "what are the odds of this showing up directly in our path by accident?"

"Not high," Gareth admitted.

Lager stepped a little closer, lowered his voice. "So maybe we leave. Maybe we use instruments to take a remote sweep from *Sabre* as we continue on our way."

It wasn't an unreasonable suggestion. Gareth had the safety of his own crew to consider.

But this wreck was an anomaly, and a violent one at that. If they didn't investigate, if they didn't find out what this was—and who had done it, if possible—it would absolutely happen again. It was their duty.

Gareth shook his head. "There could be information about what occurred here. If it was recent, there may even be an escape pod hiding in that thing's shadow. Survivors."

With the wreck so still, it was impossible to see what might be tucked away on the far side, and there was too much debris hanging around the crescent to trust the scanners entirely. They needed a scout team to get closer and do a sweep.

"Or there may be a very well-laid trap," Lager said. "Perhaps the same trap that the *Dirk* encountered."

Gareth knew it. But the *Dirk* was nowhere in sight, and the point of the Fleet was to take chances like this to prevent others from stumbling into trouble. If anyone was equipped to deal with traps and triggers, his soldiers were.

Besides, if this wreck held any clues about the whereabouts of the missing corvette, they needed to find them.

"You know we need to investigate anyway, Lieutenant," Gareth said.

Lager sighed. It was protocol, and the man knew protocol. He also knew when to question it, a quality Gareth appreciated.

Sometimes, though, Gareth had to wonder why Lager had joined up in the first place.

"And when you say 'we,'" Lager said, "you mean a team of your very competent and well-trained soldiers—"

"And me. You read my mind, Lieutenant."

Gareth wasn't in the habit of sending his soldiers into

dangerous situations when he wasn't willing to go himself. He knew it wasn't the norm, knew what his father would have said—with dismay in his tone, and definite disapproval —but he didn't care. He had to do it.

Lager folded his arms across his chest. "Sir. It's my job to protest that decision."

"Noted." Gareth clapped him on the shoulder. "Take command of the bridge, Lieutenant. I'm going in."

———

With half a dozen soldiers equipped to run a close-proximity hazard scan on the wreck, plus a pilot to remain on board, the shuttle felt like tight accommodations. But Gareth was used to the sardine-like seating, the rustles and clicks of soldiers arranging their gear and prepping the helmets they held in their laps. If not for the sobering circumstances, he'd even relish it. His entire adolescence had been a series of comings and goings on these ships.

The shuttle was another protocol mandate; don't send the frigate in close to something that might explode, and keep the majority of your personnel well away from anything questionable or mysterious. Lager would argue, surely, that the majority of personnel should include their Commander.

Maybe he wasn't wrong. But Gareth couldn't do it.

The soldier next to him looked unfamiliar, which likely meant he was new. Gareth might not be able to name every single recruit on his three-thousand soldier ship, but he spent enough time in training sessions to know their faces.

This soldier looked calm enough, hands relaxed around the edges of his helmet as he held it in his lap, but there were spots of red on his cheeks that suggested more nerves than he was letting on.

"*Sabre* hasn't done a wreck sweep in quite some time," Gareth said. "A year, maybe. Bet it's new to you."

The soldier turned and looked at him for a long moment, lips pursed. He had a light spray of freckles across his face, a lock of reddish-brown hair sweeping over his forehead. "I'm capable, if that's what you're asking."

Captain Pitorski leaned forward across the narrow aisle, as far as her straps would allow, a thin fringe of blonde bangs falling across her forehead. "Forgot your 'sir' there, Sands."

"Sorry, ma'am." He glanced at Gareth. "I joined up the last time *Sabre* was on Cadence."

A couple of months ago, then. It'd been a while since they'd done maintenance and shore leave in Cadence, which meant this one was about as green as they came. Not a usual choice for a shuttle mission.

"In that case, we're glad to have you," Gareth said.

Sands lifted a shoulder, like it wasn't anything to him. "Pay's good," he said. "Sir."

Gareth glanced at Pitorski, whose eyes were narrowed at Sands, like she was considering cuffing him in the ear. "He's observant," she said. "Thought he'd be a good one to train for scout crew."

Judging by the pinched look on her face, she might be regretting that. Sands seemed to have a fairly large chip embedded in his shoulder, but Gareth supposed that didn't automatically negate the observant part.

Sands twisted his helmet around in his lap, betraying at least a hint of buried nerves. "Who's in charge out there, anyway? It's confusing, that the Commander is coming along."

If he'd been around longer, he'd be used to that. The rest of the soldiers were elbowing each other and shaking their heads, possibly anticipating whatever dressing down Pitorski would be giving Sands when they all returned. Whatever they thought of their Commander's presence, it was nothing new to them.

"If you don't add a 'sir' to that question, soldier, I'm going to leave you out there," Pitorski said.

Sands actually rolled his eyes. "Sorry. Sir."

For the most part, crew discipline was something Gareth's officers dealt with. Major issues crossed his desk—physical altercations, desertions, harassment—but he himself dealt almost exclusively with officers.

Most soldiers weren't bold enough to unleash their acid tongues on him directly. Most officers weren't, either. If Sands kept this up, he might find out why.

"Captain Pitorski's the scouting expert," Gareth said mildly. "She's in command of the mission."

"All right," Sands said. "Sir."

When they reached the wreck, Pitorski rattled off pairs, and had the audacity to partner Gareth with Sands, and without so much as a shrug of apology. He gave her his best 'What did I ever do to you?' look, but she just shook her head. It was good practice to pair the rookie with the most seasoned veteran, and he knew it.

Luckily, Sands mostly kept his mouth shut as they used their rockets to navigate the exterior of the wreck, leaving a deep perimeter to shield them from the various unknowns that surrounded it. Pitorski's voice echoed into their head-sets, radioing data readings back to *Sabre* as their helmets recorded what they were seeing. She'd sent a team above the wreck for an initial scan and headed below it with her own partner while Gareth and Sands circled the lateral perimeter.

Up close, the wreck was far worse than it had appeared from *Sabre*'s bridge. The hull looked almost carved, like it'd been obliterated by burning rounds of electron-based cannon fire. Rare, because of the power it required to run, but not unheard of. Bits of metal glinted in the surrounding space, ranging in size from a fingernail to a decent-sized rowboat, every sliver as frozen as the hull it'd come from.

There were no bodies, that he could see.

Gareth had investigated accidents and pirate attacks, the aftermath of cartel battles. Hell, he'd just come from Halorin, where his lightning cables had halted dozens of ships in one sweep, leaving their pilots ripe for plucking and tossing in the brig.

But nothing truly *stopped* in space. Things twisted. They orbited. And with nothing to slow them down, they kept going. Wrecks didn't stay together like this. They didn't freeze like they'd been fixed into some kind of grisly diorama.

"It's just really fucking creepy," Sands said after a few minutes of silence. "It looks *wrong*."

"I can't disagree with that," Gareth said.

Sands gunned his rocket. "I'm going to swerve in closer."

"Negative, Sands," Pitorski said through the comms. "We need to send in probes."

Sands gave that patented eye roll of his. And then he fired his rockets again. "We're within reach, Captain. I can grab that silver of debris, bring it back for analysis."

There were a dozen reasons to object against any of those actions—not least the fact that they did not bring physics-defying scraps of metal back to their ship until they knew *why* said scraps defied physics—but Sands clearly wasn't considering any of that.

"Are you out of your mind?" Pitorski said. "That is a *negative*, Sands. The bridge officers gave us a perimeter. We stay outside the energy field."

Sands was already moving. Gareth tried to catch hold of his belt, but Sands was rocketing in the direction of the wreck, Pitorski cursing orders in his ear to stop.

And then, suddenly, he did. But not because Pitorski wanted him to.

Arms outstretched, Sands hit the perimeter of the wreck—the invisible line they'd been avoiding so far—fingertips first. Instead of entering the field, though, his fingers hit an invisible wall, one that seemed to grab hold of his hand and hold on fast. With his rockets still firing, Sands' hand stuck in the field, and his legs floated up over his head, turning him in an impossible somersault and flipping his back to the wreck.

He looked like an insect caught in an invisible glue trap. One that had sucked him straight in. Even the rocket fire from his pack had frozen, the streams of directional gases locked in place. It looked like a child's costume version of a Fleet uniform, complete with ribbons tied to the back of the pack.

Gareth changed position, flipping so that his head was in line with Sands'. The kid might've been all swagger on the shuttle, but his eyes were wide now, his jaw working soundlessly as sweat poured down his cheeks. At least his face could move. Was the helmet protecting him from the effects of the field?

"Commander," Pitorski said. "What's happening?"

"He's stuck at the edge of the..." Gareth trailed off, searching for a word to describe what was happening to the soldier. "It's like a stasis field of some kind. I think I can reach him."

"Negative, sir. Coors and I are coming around now. We'll be there shortly."

But Sands was starting to panic, his breath coming in gasping sobs—Gareth couldn't hear him, but he could see the man's chest heaving inside his suit. They had plenty of air, but Sands was going to make himself pass out.

The forcefield was at his back. As far as Gareth could see, the soldier's front half was still facing the freedom of open space. So he took a chance.

He reached for Sands' hand, catching it in his suited one, and pulled.

For a second, he felt like he'd plunged beneath the surface of a black ocean. Everything blurred around him, sound muting in his ears—the whuff of the oxygen, the sound of Pitorski's voice—and yet...and yet he could feel the wreck like he was a part of it, like he lived inside the metal, the smell of charred aluminum reaching his nose even though there was no way it could, no way it *should,* not with the suit pumping air through the tanks on his back.

He couldn't move his legs. He spoke, trying to activate his rockets, but no sound came out.

When he met Sands' eyes, the soldier had tears tracking down his cheeks.

A flood of whispers rose in Gareth's ears, trailing down the back of his neck like an icy fingertip, and his body tried to flinch away from the sound. The voices were wordless and breathy, muttering. He shut his eyes, trying to listen, trying to make out a word he might understand. They flowed away like a wave on the beach, then flowed back. Like they were scanning him. Investigating.

Something grasped his belt from behind, and with a

violent jerk, Gareth fell back out into normal space. He gripped Sands by the hand, refusing to let go, and the thing that had caught hold of him stalled.

For a moment, he thought they'd tear Sands in half before the field let him go. But then, with a wrenching pull, the soldier came free, and the underwater feeling drained out of Gareth's head. The burned aluminum scent was gone, and the voices along with it.

Pitorski flipped him around, and he could see that she'd used a probe to wrench them out by attaching its claws to his belt and gunning the engine.

How long had he been captured in the field? It had felt like mere seconds—not even a full minute. But she'd had time to retrieve a probe. It had to have been longer.

Gareth swallowed hard, glad his back was still facing the wreck. He didn't want to look at it again. "Good thinking, Captain," he said.

Her nostrils were flared, spots of angry red on her cheeks. When she spoke, it sounded like an accusation. "That might not have worked."

Before Gareth could respond, she turned away to usher Sands—who was openly sobbing now—back to the shuttle.

CHAPTER 5

HILDA MIGHT HAVE HAD a point about Vin's lack of resources.

In the last day, Sloane had found a grand total of two old news articles among Vin's resources that named Damian Riddle. One was a release notice from some prison in the Fringe. The second was an old bounty, no doubt expired by now. The poster's ident was obscured, so that was a dead end, too.

The longer the hours ticked by, the clearer it became that she was going to have to face Oliver's room eventually, after all.

If she did have to dig through Oliver's things, she'd really rather not be caught doing it. She wasn't sure she could deal with Hilda's 'I told you so' right now. Though with Ivy sleeping in the room, it might be tough to hide in any case.

The only other clue—if she could even call it that—was an obscure comic book by an anonymous author that followed the adventures of a hero named Damian Riddle. Who was so unbelievably perfect that Sloane had the sneaking suspicion that Damian Riddle, whoever he was, might have penned the thing himself.

She was so close to beating her head against Vin's abandoned console that she was actually almost relieved to hear raised voices in the hall. Not that she wanted a fight, but anything that could break the monotony of failure—and delay a trip to Oliver's room—would be a relief.

When she opened the door, half ready to pull her stunner in case of trouble, Brighton and Alex were facing each other down in the hall. Alex had to tip her head back to meet the security officer's eyes, but she was glaring at him like she intended to challenge him to a duel. Or maybe like they'd already started one.

"How hard is it to rinse a dish and place it in the cycler?" Brighton was asking. "You finish your breakfast. You run water. You put it in. Three steps."

Alex tipped her chin up even further, though Sloane thought if she did that again she might find herself in a staring contest with the ceiling, instead of with Brighton. "The bowl was *soaking*."

"Cereal bowls don't need to soak, Ms. Science."

"They do if little bits of cereal get stuck in them and harden so that the cycler doesn't take them off and then you need to run it again."

"Yeah, you know when that happens, though? When you don't *put your dishes in the cycler right away*."

Interesting. Sloane really would not have pegged Brighton as the neatnik of the group.

Alex opened her mouth to respond, possibly with an expletive, and Sloane slipped out of Vin's room to insert herself between her crew members before they started throwing punches. "Okay, calm down. You're going to wake Ivy."

Brighton pointed a meaty finger at Alex. "This place is going to get bugs."

"We're in *space*," Alex said. "There are no bugs in space."

Brighton actually bent sideways to glare at Alex around Sloane. These hallways had felt like a palace when Sloane was a kid. Now, they were starting to feel pretty cramped. "Planets have bugs, and we land on planets."

"Excuse the interruption!" BRO chimed in. Probably to tell them that ships could have bugs, accompanied by an irrelevant description of the computer virus that had almost taken him down last week.

"By all means, interrupt," Sloane said, "Unless you have an opinion on the argument, in which case go do some math or something."

"I do have an opinion! Dishes should go directly in the cycler! Otherwise, bits get caught in my teeth!"

"Great," Alex muttered, "even the deranged AI is against me."

"But that's not why I'm rudely interrupting," BRO said. "You have a call from Striker!"

Sloane groaned. She'd much rather discuss her crew's housekeeping habits than talk to the leader of the Cosmic Trade Federation. She didn't know if he was *the* leader, only that he was *a* leader, and that she'd pissed him off.

"Tell him I'm not home."

"Actually," Hilda's voice joined BRO's through the ceiling speakers, "you should really take the call."

Sometimes Sloane had to question whether or not she could truly be considered the captain of this ship. "Because?"

"Well, mainly because Striker's *here*."

That really was not what Sloane wanted to hear. Swallowing a curse, she pushed past Brighton. "If you punch each other over dishes, I'll have BRO recite the cycler manual to you until you memorize it."

"Ooh!" BRO said. "Can I do that anyway?"

"No. Brighton, go staff the guns, just in case."

They'd been hanging on the outskirts of the Torrent System after their adventure on Scope, mainly because there was no need to go running off across the galaxy before they knew exactly where they were headed next. But Sloane had asked Hilda to be ready to go anywhere, which meant the view from the pilot's deck was mostly taken up by the blue-green ebb of the Torrent Current, its sparkle a dominant streak across the void.

Hilda was rigid in her pilot's seat, her green parakeet perched on her left shoulder. As Sloane joined them, it hopped onto the pilot's head, chirped, then started to climb down her braid.

"Haven't seen your bird for a while," Sloane said as she dropped into the co-pilot's seat. "Glad he's back."

Hilda was frowning at her flight console, like she was cramming before a big test. Or a big escape. "Back from where? A vacation in the bands? He was in my room."

"Why?"

"Are you going to talk to your Federation friend—whose weapons are hot, by the way—or are you going to ask a million questions about where my budgie's been?"

"Why not both?" Sloane strapped in and dialed open the communication board. Unfortunately, there was indeed a sleek looking Federation ship looming in the distance. It looked about the size of *Moneymaker*, though appearances could be deceiving. The sides were painted black, reminding Sloane of the relentless dark shine of the streets that ran through Federation's home city, Obsidian.

"Striker," Sloane said. "Nice to see you again. My pilot's telling me your weapons are hot, but I thought she must be mistaken. Since you and I are such good friends and all. You know how pilots are. So alarmist."

Hilda shot Sloane a look that would have sent most kids scuttling off to finish their homework.

"Ms. Tarnish." Striker's voice came back smooth and clear, like he was calling in from the next room over. He sounded so refined. Not at all like a man whose ship was posturing like it intended to blow them to bits very soon. "I may not have been clear when we spoke before. Perhaps we had a miscommunication."

Sloane raised her eyebrows and matched Striker's tone. "Perhaps."

"Stop trying to sound fancy," Hilda hissed.

"Why? I'm good at it."

"No, you sound like you're making fun of him."

Sloane didn't think that was true, but fine. She did seem to fit in better with the outlaw set than she ever had with Dad's fancy friends on Elter.

"I asked you to deliver Brighton Walsh to Halorin System," Striker continued. "But it appears that he's still on your ship."

"Oh, that," Sloane said, doing her best to keep her tone light. She'd gotten pretty far in life by playing up the flighty angle, though she had a feeling Striker could see through it. Commander Fortune definitely had. "Maybe you didn't hear, but we were attacked by Fox Clan ships. Funnily enough, they came after us from a hiding spot on Federation Planet. I've been meaning to ask, do you have any thoughts on that?"

Hilda rubbed her fingertips across her forehead. "This was not how I wanted to die."

"Hiding on Federation," Striker repeated. "Is that what your Fleet Commander claimed?"

Well, yes. Sloane wanted to say she didn't take Fortune at his word, but in a way, she kind of did. The man was almost naively honest, as far as she'd seen, though she hadn't completely ruled out the possibility that he was a very good actor with bad intentions. That was definitely what Vin had seemed to believe.

But mostly, she believed Fortune because he'd been in Federation System when she'd left it—perfectly placed to watch the chase in real time—and the Fox Clan ships had accosted her as soon as she'd left the Current. The evidence fit.

It was possible the ships could have been hiding on Federation, or somewhere in Pike System, without Striker knowing. It didn't seem likely, though. The man knew so much about what went on in the galaxy, it seemed impossible that he could miss trespassers in his own territory.

Sloane didn't intend to take sides in the rivalry between the Federation and the Fleet. Or between Striker and Fortune, who hated each other with the badly concealed rage of men who felt it would be bad form to openly admit the depth of their desire to crush each other's heads.

Where was Fortune now, anyway? Off dealing with important Fleet stuff. More important than a wayward bounty hunter, certainly. There wasn't any reason she should have heard from him after they'd fought together in Halorin System. But for some reason, she wished she had.

"I'm willing to board now," Striker said, without waiting for her take on Fortune's honesty. He already knew the answer, anyway. "I'll take Brighton into custody myself, and we'll go our separate ways. No weapons, no harm done."

"Yeah, no. Sorry. He's my security officer now."

There was a pause. As if Striker was absorbing information that, in all likelihood, he already knew. "Brighton Walsh is a dangerous man who's wanted in several systems."

And a loyally protective neatnik who got annoyed by dirty dishes. "Oh yeah? Why does Halorin get him, then? Did they bid highest?"

Hilda buried her face in her hands.

"The Federation doesn't answer to you, Ms. Tarnish. Allow us to board, or we'll open fire."

Hilda sighed. "Oh, well. Brighton was good while he lasted."

"Brighton," Sloane said, "shoot at him."

"Gladly."

Hilda sighed again. "How did I know that was coming?"

"Because you know I wouldn't turn over a member of my crew. I mean Vin's crew."

Hilda shot Sloane a side glance, which she chose to ignore. "Uh huh."

A pair of bright red streaks lit up the space between *Moneymaker* and the Federation ship, bursting against Striker's hull like rogue fireworks.

"Make for the Current," Sloane said.

Hilda's fingers danced on the dashboard, her lips twisted in concentration. And maybe a sliver of disagreement. "That is a temporary solution."

"But the safest one until we know where we're headed."

Sloane half expected Striker to comm her again with another jab, but maybe he knew the time for snide comments had passed. As *Moneymaker* zoomed for the Current, Sloane shifted the view to the rear cameras just in time to see the Federation ship light up with a double set of red lights. They looked like eyes.

And then they looked like death, as the lasers chased *Moneymaker* toward the Current. "Brace," Sloane said, and the hits rocked into the shields like flaming-hot boulders.

The shields held. Sloane gripped the arms of her chair. "Are we Current worthy?"

"Barely." Hilda's teeth were clamped together, and the word hissed out from between them.

"Then in we go."

The Federation guns lit up again, and Sloane pictured Striker standing on the flight deck, wearing his signature leather vest and preparing to murder her because she'd failed to deliver a bounty. And maybe a little bit because in doing so, she'd also rejected his offer to come work for the Federation.

Still, he was willing to kill her, and her crew, over a couple of slights. How important was Brighton, anyway? What had he done to incur this kind of wrath from the Federation?

The question rang out in her mind as the blue wash of the Current closed around Moneymaker, dragging them into the only safe zone in the galaxy.

CHAPTER 6

AS SOON AS Gareth's feet hit *Sabre*'s decks, he issued the order to head out to the asteroid mine. Unless the pirates who'd blown up the hauler had gone speeding back to the Current, HTR-79 was the next logical destination.

And even if the pirates weren't there—Gareth decided to think of these attackers as pirates—the asteroid mine had missed a water delivery. They might need assistance.

Sabre would leave a warning barrier in place around the wreck, at least until they could get a pair of corvettes out here to block off the area and investigate further. Gareth would have stayed to stand guard it himself, but *Sabre* needed to reach the asteroid, and to make sure the people who lived and worked in the mine were safe.

Though pirates typically plundered. As far as he could tell, these ones had only destroyed.

Lager fell into step beside him as he made his way up to the bridge, his cheeks flushed. Gareth had the sense that the Lieutenant had rushed down here to meet him so he could try to talk him into doing something sensible before he had to act more like an officer than a friend.

"You need to go to the infirmary, sir," Lager said.

Gareth couldn't stop the corner of his mouth from lifting, just a touch. So predictable. "No need. Sands is headed there now."

"And you were caught in that stasis field, too. We don't know what effect it might have had."

Gareth didn't understand how the field had extended like that, how it had wrapped around him—and not, as far as he could tell, around Pitorski's probe—but Lager wasn't wrong. It had captured him just as fully as it had Sands.

"I appreciate that, Lager," Gareth said, "and I promise I'll get checked out later. But for now, I need to get up to the bridge."

Lager put a hand on his arm, and Gareth paused. His knees felt shaky, it was true, and his ears were ringing a bit, but there'd be time enough to deal with that later.

"If you want to know why your soldier disobeyed orders out there," Lager said, his voice little louder than a whisper, "consider the example you're setting. That was *reckless*. And *you* disobeyed the mission leader's orders. Either you're Commander when you're out there, or you're not. Once your feet leave the ship, sir, the decision needs to hold."

Gareth wasn't sure he'd ever seen Lager angry before. Not really. But his friend's eyes were flashing with something that edged close to rage, his lips pressed thin, his hands pressed flat against his sides. And, Gareth had to admit, for good reason.

"You're right," Gareth said. "I set a poor example. I apologize, Lieutenant."

Lager blinked, clearly surprised not to be entering an argument. "Don't apologize to me. Apologize to Pitorski."

"I will. Thank you for being candid, Lieutenant."

Lager let out a breath. "Thanks for not throwing me in the brig, sir."

Not Gareth's style, and Lager knew it. Besides, Gareth had told Sands himself that Pitorski would be in command for the mission. Lager was right, and Gareth would be a jerk —not to mention a fool—if he ignored that.

Lieutenant Stills met them at the door as they entered the bridge. "You've got a live call in the strat room, sir," she said.

Gareth beckoned Lager to follow him in, fully expecting another intelligence update from Captain West on the whereabouts of the *Dirk*. No use in keeping Lager out of the call when Gareth would only relay everything to him, anyway. West must have made his way to a Current so they could speak in real time. Maybe that meant he had some useful information to share.

But West wasn't waiting for him in the strat room. Instead, it was Alisa March who looked out at them from the wall screen. Alisa tended to opt for screens over holos; she always said the bluish tint made her look old.

Today, she looked tired and pale, her already thin face drawn nearly to gauntness. Dark circles puffed out from under her eyes, and her usually tidy red hair was tied back with a cloth headband.

She looked raw with exhaustion, like she'd just escaped from captivity, yet Gareth couldn't help his relief at seeing her. Some part of him had been sure that Osmond Clay had had her murdered.

"Alisa," he said. "You don't know how glad I am to see you. Are you all right? I've been trying to contact you for days."

She must be traveling in-Current, to be facing them for a live call. Like Captain West, Alisa tended to do that when dealing with important matters. When she folded her hands on the table in front of her, Gareth could see they were shaking. "I didn't want to believe it of you, Gareth."

Gareth frowned. Beside him, Lager shifted his weight slightly between his feet. Gareth wondered if he knew what Alisa meant. "Believe what?"

"You want me to say it?" Alisa might look like she hadn't slept since the FAC coup, but her voice was as hard as a steel blade. A steel blade that was pointed directly at Gareth's face. "The Fleet's making a run at establishing a galactic empire. Not that I need to tell you that."

Gareth wanted to laugh, except for the sick feeling that roiled through his stomach. "You never put any stock in that stale old rumor."

"Then where are you hiding your corvettes?" Her voice was a clip, cold and dry. She *did* believe it. The sick feeling in his stomach turned cold, like something dark and painful was taking root there. How could she?

"First the *Dirk* goes missing," she said, as if that were evidence, "and now the *Hunter*."

The *Hunter*? The *Hunter* was assigned to Adu, had been patrolling there for months, keeping an eye on the cartels.

Gareth looked at Lager, who already had his fliptab in his palm, lines of intel flickering by in streams of blue. After a beat, he blinked, then nodded without looking up. "How could you know that?" Lager asked. "*We* didn't know."

Alisa's eyes were narrowed, as if she were trying to see through an act or a ruse. Gareth had visited this woman's home in Torrent as a child, had gone running through the estate's summer meadows chasing butterflies. She'd stood beside him at his father's funeral.

"So you think I'm what, some kind of evil mastermind?"

It took a concerted effort to keep his voice clear and calm. If one of his longtime allies believed this tripe—maybe his staunchest ally and friend, outside of the Fleet itself—then who else did? The Halorin System governors, perhaps?

Alisa stared into the camera, unblinking. "I took it upon myself to investigate rumors of a Fleet base on Olton Moon. In Adu System. Gareth would never put boots on the ground without authorization, I told myself. He'd hold to the accords." She leaned forward. "You know what I found?"

Gareth had a feeling he could guess. "My missing corvettes?"

"No, though I have to assume you're hiding them in a similarly illegal corner of the galaxy. My ambassadors found so many Fleet ships guarding Olton Moon that they couldn't even land. They were turned away with threats that I can recite in my sleep, I've listened to the recordings so many times."

Sloane had accused him of the same thing. He'd nearly forgotten it, in the aftermath of the Fox Clan fight, but her ship had tried to land on Olton Moon to avoid the cartel once before. And they'd been chased away by a squad of cube ships.

But Gareth knew every Fleet base by heart. He knew the temporary ones his father had authorized by request, and the temporary ones he'd set up himself. He knew where the Fleet operated on Cadence, its three main bases and several small outposts. And he could name every civilian contractor they'd ever done business with; some were scattered across the galaxy, true, but they were fully legal.

The Fleet had its secrets, but they kept to the accords. There was no Fleet base on Olton Moon.

Gareth drew in a breath. "Alisa, I'm being set up here. You know me."

"I thought I did." Her voice was a quiver. Grief? Barely restrained rage? He couldn't tell. "How long has this been going on? Your father, was he involved?"

Heat burst through Gareth's chest, and he forced it down before he opened his mouth to speak. His father's heart would break at the suggestion, but it wouldn't help the situation if Gareth responded in anger. "Osmond Clay is a weasel who would murder me at the first opportunity." All right, maybe a little anger. "Osmond Clay—"

"Clay's saving your ass," Alisa interrupted. "The galaxy's ready to revolt. He gave this Olton Moon intel to the Commission, and three quarters of us resigned on the spot. Myself included."

That did explain the Halorin governors' response to him, then, and their demands to speak with the Commission. "If the Commission suspected that we'd broken the accords, it would have been their duty to respond to the situation," Gareth said. "To call us to task."

"What do you think that summit is for? Clay's going to strip you of power."

Gareth shook his head. "Why join the Commission if you meant to walk away at the first sign of trouble? The point of the FAC is to ensure that the Fleet follows the guidelines."

"This was never a problem before."

Cowards, every single one of them. He wasn't the one who'd betrayed his post; they were. Before Gareth could decide whether to say as much, Alisa pointed a finger at him. "You'd better find a way to show up at that summit, or I'll be the least of your concerns."

No. He had a feeling this conversation would linger in

his heart whether he wanted it to or not. Gareth glanced at Lager, whose lips were parted, eyebrows raised.

"I'd like nothing more." Gareth chose his words carefully, speaking slowly. It would be too easy to let his anger bubble to the surface. "But I'm not invited."

"That isn't Clay's story." Alisa dropped her hand, then blinked rapidly as if she was trying not to cry in front of him. As if she were the one who'd been betrayed.

Whatever Clay had said to the FAC, whatever he'd shown them, Alisa believed it. And she'd done her own investigation. She *did* think she'd been betrayed.

"Alisa," Gareth said, "I've only ever wanted to keep the peace. It was all Dad ever wanted."

"Then he'd be ashamed."

He would be. If it were true, then yes, he would be.

Just the thought of establishing an empire, the scale of it...the accusation was a running joke among officers. Can you imagine the overhead? The recruitment efforts? The Fleet might be powerful, but they'd been intentionally restricted over the years.

But *someone* was building Fleet-style ships and sending them to Olton Moon. And it did seem, at first glance, that only someone in the Fleet would be able to replicate their exact specs. It was possible, wasn't it, that one of his people was at least involved? There were tens of thousands of soldiers scattered on ships throughout the galaxy. Gareth kept track of them as best he could, but soldiers retired. They retreated to unknown corners. He couldn't know everyone.

Doubt wavered in his chest, and he made himself take a breath while Alisa watched, eyes glittering.

He took a second breath and tried again. "I'd never try

to establish an empire in the galaxy, Alisa. You have to know that."

"I saw it, Gareth," she said. "I'm not buying into some bullshit heresy. I saw your ships with my own eyes. If they don't belong to the Fleet, then whose are they?"

"I don't know. But we need to find out."

"Then I suggest you get to the summit and convince the FAC that the investigation is worth the trouble. Goodbye, Gareth."

Before Gareth could say another word, she ended the call. He scrubbed a hand across his face and dropped into the nearest chair. His knees felt weak, his body aching with the effort of the conversation. Maybe he should visit the infirmary after all.

"The *Hunter*?" he asked.

"Vanished," Lager confirmed. "Last beam came out of Adu."

Gareth looked up. Lager still had his fliptab in his hand, but he was watching Gareth with an almost stricken look on his face, his eyes wide, brows edging toward his hairline.

"*You* don't think I'm trying to establish a galactic empire, do you?" Gareth asked.

"No, sir. You're terrible at hiding things. And besides, you'd need my help for something of that scale."

"The paperwork alone..."

Lager didn't smile, and Gareth didn't blame him.

"All right," Gareth said, "I can't go after two missing ships at once. We'll need to redirect one of the frigates out of Adu System to go looking for the *Hunter*."

Lager planted his feet wide, like he was afraid whatever he was about to say might earn him a punch him in the nose. He'd gotten away with calling Gareth insubordinate, and less than half and hour ago, so Gareth couldn't predict what would be worrying him now.

"I think you should send me after the *Hunter*," Lager said.

Gareth considered this. "There are three frigates patrolling in Adu right now. It'd be easier to divert one of them."

"Yes, sir, but their hands are plenty full. I can take a team in a cube ship or a shuttle."

Cube ships carried two comfortably, three miserably. Hardly a team. They had weapons, yes, but the lightning nets were only marginally useful without a group of cubes to operate them, and the guns were minimal by necessity. The ships were designed to fit back into a frigate or to lock together to transport larger groups. They were light, and they were fast, but they rarely patrolled without a frigate to watch over them.

"Corvettes are going missing, Lager," Gareth said. "I don't want you skipping around in a cube ship."

"Cubes are small, and they're difficult to track."

Gareth propped his elbow on the table, fighting a wave of fatigue. "And they're *vulnerable*."

Lager threw his hands up. "Then send a dozen cube ships. But send me with them."

Gareth pushed down against the table, grounding his elbow against the hard surface. "You're going to have to convince me why I should send my right-hand officer away right at the exact moment that everything's going to hell."

Lager moved away from the door and came to sit next to Gareth at the table, meeting his eyes with unflinching conviction. The man was nothing if not persistent. "*Because* I'm your right hand, sir. Someone's out there making Fleet-style ships, and I know you don't want to believe this, but it could well be someone in the Fleet. Because Striker knew about our stealth hulls, and where to find us. And because our ships keep disappearing into nothing. You need someone out there you can trust."

Gareth trusted his soldiers, and his officers. But he couldn't deny Lager's point; he didn't want to think any of them could be involved in this—what were they doing on Olton Moon, that needed to be defended as if by the Fleet? —but it would be foolish to automatically absolve his people of suspicion.

Gareth drew in a long breath, then let it out. "Jim's going to kill me."

"My husband understands the job," Lager said mildly. "You can't keep everyone safe, sir."

Gareth huffed out a breath of agreement. Maybe Jim understood the job better than he did himself. "All right, I'll relay the orders," he said. "I'm not sure who'll keep me honest with you gone."

Lager grinned. "Don't worry," he said, "I'm training Sands."

CHAPTER 7

FOR SOMEONE who'd supposedly been operating as an outlaw since before Sloane's birth, Uncle Vin had frustratingly few dubious resources—black markets, underground corners of the feeds, etc.—linked to his console. Sloane had asked Brighton to crack open an encrypted part of the computer, and it had allowed her to access a few useful feeds, but not a single one of them said a peep about Damian Riddle.

Of everything she'd encountered, the comic book contained the most mentions. Sloane had read it four times, combing the story for clues, but there was no hidden data, no message she could tease out. And the story was completely ridiculous.

After another wasted day of poking through nonsense, she had to admit the truth. She needed to search through Oliver's console.

Oliver had been the true criminal among them: a Fleet deserter, a thief, and a frequent guest at the Parse Galaxy's hidden black markets. She'd known it, even before he'd betrayed her, yet she'd still put her crew in danger by bringing him on board. And then, because those screwups weren't enough, she'd decided that sleeping with him would be an extra good idea.

But he'd been charming and knowledgeable, a little bit dangerous, and Sloane had been lost.

Sloane had heard Hilda telling Ivy that they might need to borrow her cabin, even after Sloane's insistence that it wouldn't be necessary. Still, maybe Sloane wouldn't have to admit she'd gone in. She could hear Ivy's voice upstairs in the kitchen, hopefully not mediating a fight about dish-doing. Sloane could slip in, bang around on the console for a while, find a clue about Damian's whereabouts, and slip back out.

With a deep breath, she opened the door.

The slim pack Ivy had brought with her was propped on the bed, and the room smelled fresher than the last time Sloane had ventured in here. But there was still so much to remember. So much to regret.

Ivy wasn't even the first guest to stay in this room. For reasons unknown, Hilda had assigned Fortune to this cabin after their jungle misadventures on Cal Cornum. Maybe she'd relished the thought of trashing Oliver's old cabin with a layer of mud. Or maybe it'd simply been the first available door.

Even with clean bedding and someone else's things, it was Oliver's space. She'd never cleared the clothes out of his drawers, never removed the poster he'd tacked on the wall above the bed. It showed a bunch of diagrams of weapons she was pretty sure were banned in most of the galaxy. The nice parts of it, anyway.

She suddenly found herself wishing she could see more of Fortune in the room, though that was a ridiculous idea. The Fleet Commander had only stayed on *Moneymaker* for a few nights. What would he have left behind? A pristine Fleet uniform and a list of grievances against her?

Pushing past the confusion that churned in her gut, Sloane started for Oliver's powered-down console, then paused.

Fortune *had* stayed here. And Fortune might actually be the answer.

He wasn't her biggest fan, it was true. But they'd helped each other more than once. And hadn't he called her capable? Exasperatingly capable, yes, but still. He'd said the word.

It wasn't that she wanted to avoid Oliver's things, a point she punctuated by forcing herself to sit down in his desk chair. It was just that Fortune knew things about the entire galaxy. He might be able to help.

If he'd respond to a direct message via eye screen, that was. He'd have to approve her request, and she was only about fifty-fifty on those odds. Maybe forty-sixty against.

She sent a contact request and held her breath, then decided that was stupid and made herself breathe until the screen lit up green. Which, to her surprise, it actually did. Before she could decide what to say—something she should have considered before she placed the call—his voice was in her ear.

"Ms. Tarnish," he said, his voice low and immediately identifiable. It had a rough edge to it, though, an almost ragged quality. Had she woken him? What kind of clock did the Fleet follow? She had no idea.

"Are you all right?" he asked.

Sloane sat back in the chair, as if he could see her. Which he couldn't. "I'm always all right, Fortune."

A pause. "I didn't think you'd contact me for less than a disaster."

Right. Had she even thanked him for his interference in Halorin? It wasn't just that he brought his big frigate to loom over her enemies, though that'd been a help, but that he'd talked her through the process of reconnecting *Moneymaker*'s guns. In the middle of a battle, when her arm had been badly injured and her nerves had been frayed to hell.

Maybe that was why this moment felt so awkward. She felt like he'd seen her—listened to her, anyway—during her most vulnerable moment, stripped bare of all her swagger and shields. She didn't know how to talk to someone who'd heard her like that. She wasn't sure she could even name anyone else who'd heard her like that. Not in this galaxy, anyway.

But he was waiting for a response, so she had to say something. She cleared her throat. "Yeah, well, I guess I was kind of hoping for your…"

She really didn't want to say *help*. Or assistance. She didn't want to admit that there was something she hadn't managed to figure out on her own. But then, she hadn't figured the guns out on her own, either, and he hadn't given her shit about that.

"Input?" he supplied.

Sloane snapped her fingers. "Yes. Input. If you're willing."

"I'm certainly curious."

"Is that the same as willing?"

"Let's say yes."

It didn't guarantee a response, but it was something. And even if he didn't know the answers, he might be able to find them. In the battle between facing Oliver's console and asking for help, this was the lesser evil. "All right," she said. "What do you know about Damian Riddle? He's…actually,

I'm not sure exactly what he is. Some kind of pirate-thief guy. Maybe a loner, maybe not."

The comic books had implied it, but it was really just subtext. She'd have to read more to find out. Not that she wanted to read more of that story. Even if the last issue had ended in a cliffhanger.

There was another pause, this one longer. "If I ask why, will you tell me?"

Sloane thought about that. She didn't want to tell Fortune everything Ivy had shared with her, though he might already know a lot of what she'd said about the Interplanetary Dwellers. "He stole something from a client," Sloane said. "The client wants it back."

"Am I to assume this bounty is not Federation approved?"

"I didn't say it was a bounty."

"Ms. Tarnish, please."

"Okay, no, it's not approved."

"Good."

Sloane blinked, surprised. A week ago, Commander Fortune would have lectured her on the risks of engaging in a bounty hunt that came without the protection of the Federation. There were rules, protocols, regulations, blah blah blah. She'd have tuned out halfway through the speech, and he'd have gotten frustrated with her and straightened his spine, tucking his hands behind his back the way he did when he was trying not to show his annoyance. Or any other emotion. Though the more time she spent with the man, the more easily she found it to read him.

Times changed quickly in the Parse Galaxy, in any case. She supposed a man like Fortune needed to keep up with those changes.

"I've been looking for information on Damian Riddle in my uncle's databases," Sloane said. "But I can't find much."

Not a lie. Not the full truth, but he knew better than to expect that of her. He wouldn't—couldn't, or so he claimed —give her the classified stuff, and she wouldn't give him the specifics of her job. Or of her reluctance to use the resources she had.

"Just a couple of badly written comic books?" Fortune asked.

He'd seen them, then. Interesting. "Yup. Art's not bad though."

And really, the story *might* be going somewhere. If there were more than two issues, she might be able to form a better opinion.

"Damian Riddle's an assumed name," Fortune said. Sloane tried to picture him—was he standing on the bridge of his ridiculously named frigate? Watching a bunch of soldiers practice zero-grav maneuvers? Maybe he was outside the ship, performing maintenance and looking out at the stars. Not that a Fleet Commander would usually perform maintenance himself.

Of course, Fleet Commanders also didn't lead ground operations, or throw themselves into danger on the regular the way Fortune did. He really needed a deeper under-standing of his job description.

Or maybe Sloane did. She was the outsider, after all. Maybe that was what was expected in Fleet-land.

"His real name is Damian Sol," Fortune added, snap-ping her back to the conversation and out of her daydreams about his surroundings. "He's the son of the casino magnate."

"Archimedes Sol?"

"That's the one."

"Huh. I tried to rob him once."

Fortune let out a breath that sounded like a laugh. "Who haven't you tried to rob?"

"I've tried to rob everyone."

Another breath. Yes, that was definitely a laugh. "Well, we know Sol's got a place on Scope. I wouldn't be surprised if he's carved out a niche for himself in Adu System, too, but I'd start there."

"Ugh, I was just in Scope. It's so..." She trailed off, searching for the right word to capture the intense *nothingness* of the city. At least, what had been intense nothingness, before she'd walked straight into an active firefight.

"Beige?" he suggested.

She was surprised he'd noticed. "Yes."

"Sorry to disappoint. You're in-Current now?"

"Affirmative, Commander sir." It occurred to her that she could tell him about how the Federation had tried to kill her, but it might be better not to bother him with that. She really didn't need his bully-sized frigate coming to her rescue. He had other things to do, and besides, he had a bit of a tendency to get in her way.

Fortune did know a lot about Riddle, though, and off the top of his head, too. Must've gone chasing after the guy at some point. She tapped her fingers on her knee. "Fleet never caught Riddle, huh?"

Fortune was quiet for a long moment, and she wondered if she'd offended him somehow. Was he the kind of person who held onto grudges, or took it personally when a criminal escaped his self-righteous clutches?

Maybe he was just the kind of person who held himself accountable for his mistakes. "It's a big galaxy," she added.

"He hasn't been a priority." She could hear the careful way he said the words, like he was plucking each one deliberately off its shelf, and she found that she really wanted to know why. Maybe it was simply that he thought through his responses before allowing them out of his mouth.

An actual filter. What would it be like to have one of those?

"Is he slippery?" she asked, folding her feet up under her thighs to sit cross-legged on Oliver's chair. "Tough to catch? Maybe bested you once or twice?"

"Actually," he said, "I think I'd pay to see you two go head-to-head."

"I'll be sure to get a video."

The conversation should be over; she had what she needed, and he was a busy Fleet Commander. She shouldn't take any more of his time than she already had. Not that that had ever stopped her in the past, but he had helped her.

And yet...and yet, she couldn't quite bring herself to end the connection between them. Direct communication across the galaxy was rare enough, the Currents allowing for it when other spots didn't. Sometimes, though, it made her feel far away from everything, more isolated than ever. He could be on the other side of the galaxy by now, back in Adu or out in the Fringe Systems. She licked her lips, listening to him breathe, goodbye on the tip of her tongue.

Instead, she heard herself say something else. What was the good of a fritzing filter, if you didn't let it follow its gut? "So," she said, doing her best to sound casual, "how are things going in Halorin?"

CHAPTER 8

WITH SABRE en route to asteroid mine HTR-79, Gareth had been trying to coax his body into sleeping for a few hours. He'd said goodbye to Lager, dutifully paid a visit to the infirmary, then retreated to his bunk to rest.

So far, he'd only succeeded in staring at the ceiling of his cabin, his eyes tracing the tile seams while he tried to forget the eerie horror of the wreckage they'd left behind, the singed cuts across the hull.

Who would blow up a water hauler without bothering to plunder its contents? Water was a precious commodity, depending on where you were in the galaxy, as was the oxygen that kept the crew alive.

Many a vicious pirate had been known to strip ships of their life support stores, leaving the crew to suffocate. But why put the bones of the ship into a stasis field like that? It was as if someone had left it for him to find.

These were the questions that kept his eyes wide open. That, and the echoes of the whispers that ran through his mind like an echo, his brain straining to sort through their murmurings. What were they? A figment of his imagination, or some byproduct of the stasis field?

Over and over, his mind turned it, until sleep became a distant dream. An impossibility.

And then Sloane's name had popped up on his eye screen, a request for direct contact. And Gareth had accepted it.

Now that she'd gotten the information she needed, he expected her to sign off. Instead, she said, "How are things going in Halorin?"

She'd sounded reluctant to be contacting him in the first place, to ask for his help, and he had to wonder what dead ends she'd encountered to convince her it'd be worth the trouble.

Now, though... now she seemed almost hesitant to end the call.

Imagination. It had to be.

"I'm not in Halorin," he said. "Left *Cutlass* to deal with that mess."

"My mess, you mean."

"Fox Clan's mess."

She made a humming noise that suggested she didn't quite believe him. "Are you...but things are okay?"

Gareth propped his hand behind his head, trying to understand if there was some meaning behind the question. She'd proved she was more than willing to ask directly if she wanted to get information out of him. So why the hesitation? Was she asking if he was safe?

"Mostly fine," he said. "I was in the infirmary today." There'd been no ill effects from the stasis field that the doctors could detect; Sands had already been released.

He didn't quite know why he was telling her. He didn't quite know why she would care. If she *did* care. Maybe it was because Lager had gone, leaving Gareth alone with his Serious Commander Face and an asteroid that might or might not be overrun with pirates.

Not to mention a pair of missing corvettes, a former ally who no longer trusted him, and a galaxy that increasingly believed he wanted to install himself as their supreme emperor.

None of it felt real.

"What happened?" she asked.

Gareth blinked. His eyes were dry from lack of sleep. He should see to some drops before his next shift. "I tried to rescue one of my soldiers from a stasis field and almost got trapped myself."

A beat of silence. He tried to place her on her ship, in her cabin or down in the cargo hold where she'd kept Brighton prisoner, her hair in its usual long ponytail. "Let me picture this, Fortune," she said. "Your buddy—"

"A Fleet soldier."

"—got trapped in a stasis field, whatever that is, and you thought you could muscle your way out of it even though he couldn't?"

"That's about the size of it."

"Fortune. No."

He wasn't sure why, but the clear disapproval in her voice made him smile. She would have found some way to bring Sands back by casting a fishing line or repurposing the stasis field to eject everything, thereby accomplishing her goal while also putting her own ship in danger.

And here she was, disapproving of him. It should be annoying, but it just made him want to laugh. He'd accuse her of being a bad influence, except that this was far from the first time he'd pulled a stunt like this.

"Was that Lieutenant angry?" she asked.

She didn't miss much. She'd seen Lager what, once? And he'd been in miniature at the time, a holograph. That was it, unless she'd listened in on his private conversations. Which, he had to admit, was a distinct possibility with Sloane.

"So angry," Gareth said.

At that, she laughed. It was a delighted sound and a delightful one, full-throated and, he thought, completely unhindered. He felt his smile widening in response, and he found himself wishing—it was foolish, he knew it was—that he had business in the vicinity of Scope. Any business at all.

Before he could respond, an alert from the bridge lit up his eye screen. *Approaching HTR-79. Twenty-five-minute ETA.*

So much for sleep. But in some ways, this conversation had been better.

"I have to go," he said.

"Right," she said, reining in her merriment, and Gareth thought he'd never been so sorry. "Thanks for your help. Be safe, if that's in your vocabulary."

"Is it in yours?"

"Fair enough. Later, Fortune."

She cut the connection, leaving him alone in his cabin, looking up at the same dull ceiling he'd been staring at throughout their conversation. Only now, with her voice cut off, it was all he had left.

Gareth set the conversation aside as best he could and headed for the bay where the landing parties prepared for missions, Sloane's laughter still ringing in his ears.

Pitorski was already there, and she gave him a questioning look after greeting him with a salute. Gareth interpreted it as an *Are you going to let me do my job this time, sir?* look, and he couldn't blame her for it.

Gareth returned her salute, then joined her in prepping to launch with the landing party. No use in pretending that wasn't his intention; he needed to be there, and Lager wasn't here to caution him against it. Not that he'd listen, anyway.

"I owe you an apology, Captain," Gareth said, as they zipped atmo gear over shorts and T-shirts and ran checks on their oxygen and communication gear. "I undermined your leadership on the hauler."

Pitorski whipped her hair into a tight bun. "You're Fleet Commander, sir. You outrank me."

The words were casual enough, but her lips were pressed thin, and he'd have been willing to bet she was biting her cheek to keep from chewing him out.

Gareth held her gaze. "Not on an operation where you're the mission leader. You're the expert, and we put you in charge for a reason. *I* put you in charge for a reason. It won't happen again."

Pitorski hesitated, then nodded. "Thank you, sir."

They worked in silence for a few more minutes, prepping their gear and checking each other's with the efficient motions of soldiers who'd repeated the task a thousand times before.

When they'd finished, Gareth stepped back, anxious for the rest of the team to arrive, anxious to set foot on the asteroid. "Is Sands coming?" he asked.

"No, sir."

"Oh, thank the stars."

She grinned, then tamped it down as the rest of the landing squad joined them in the bay.

The shuttle instruments detected no stasis field surrounding the asteroid—now that they knew what it looked like, they could watch for it—but no one responded to their requests to land, either.

The shuttle entered via a narrow passage that was common in asteroid mines. Not a standard, perhaps, but frequent enough. Asteroid mines needed wide tunnels for supply imports—food, water, oxygen, equipment—as well as plenty of room to ship out their goods.

Security was typically limited if it existed at all; the bands were too isolated to draw many pirates or criminals, and miners needed active workers more than they needed security officers to stare at screens all day. Still, it was strange not to receive any communications on the ground.

They landed without an issue and stepped out into a pressurized bay, though Pitorski ordered them to keep their helmets engaged, and Gareth certainly didn't disagree with that. Unease prickled up his spine, reminding him uncomfortably of the stasis-field whispers. Nothing about this felt right.

The Captain took the lead, pairing up with another officer and assigning Gareth to the rear with a partner, which he did without complaint. He'd promised to follow orders. And if he suspected that Pitorski wanted to clear a path ahead of him through the asteroid, he couldn't fault her for it. She was perfectly capable of handling an ambush, if one came.

The interior halls of the asteroid were smooth and basic, like a puncture wound that penetrated deep into the rock. The passage was raw, utilitarian, and other than the occasional bowed stripes of steel to reinforce the tunnels—plus a scattering of coin-shaped gravity anchors to keep their feet on the ground—there was nothing but rock.

Ahead, the tunnel opened into a wide room. Pitorski started in, weapon braced against her shoulder, and Gareth heard her curse softly as she and her partner made their way fully into the room.

"Clear," she said, lowering her weapon to her waist. "Shit."

Itching to make his way to the front, Gareth followed the other soldiers into what turned out to be a cafeteria. Long metal tables dotted the room at rigid intervals, with stools attached. A serving area was bolted to the far end of the room, the top set with stacks of secured plates and dishes.

At first, Gareth couldn't see what had made Pitorski curse. And then his gaze found the bodies.

They were crumpled along the gray rock walls to either side, partially hidden by the rows of tables. Brownish blood stains washed the surrounding floor, and Gareth swallowed his horror as he stepped over to the nearest one, a man with graying hair. He wore a brown jumpsuit with mining insignia on the shoulder above a name tag: *Jag*.

These were miners. Workers. Who would murder them like this? The same people who'd stopped the hauler, surely, but they couldn't have been that far ahead of *Sabre*. How had they gotten here so quickly, given the estimated timing of the hauler attack? They must have more than one ship.

Maybe the pirates had stopped the hauler in order to keep its crew from finding this massacre. Or maybe they'd set up the stasis field to delay *Sabre* until they could carry it out. But why? Who were they?

Gareth set his scanners to search for life, for any signs of survivors. Judging by the color of the blood alone, this had happened well before their arrival. Still, he searched, swallowing back a wad of salty bile.

"They were executed," one of the soldiers said. "Look."

Gareth straightened, forcing his gaze to follow where

the man was pointing. Blood stained the rock walls at eye level, as though the people had been standing against them before being mowed down. It made him want to empty his stomach. It made him want to weep.

"We should take the elevator down to the mines," Pitorski said, pointing to the open doors of the elevator. "They might still be here."

Gareth didn't have to ask who she meant. They'd seen no ship in the vicinity, and it was difficult to hide in the bands, though not impossible. Any evidence that might lead them to the next step would be worth pursuing. As difficult as it was, they'd need to comb this rock for clues if they wanted to prevent it from happening again.

And Alisa thought they wanted to run the galaxy. Gareth would settle for never seeing a sight like this again.

They returned to the corridor, weapons ready. Pitorski had opted for Herald Class Electron Snipers, guns that ran the length of his forearm and could stun or burn depending on the setting. But nothing stirred, and they paused only to examine a tripwire someone had installed across their path. It'd already been triggered, though; the wire hung slack against the floor, and the lower section of the wall was punctured with bullet spray.

Blood trailed along the floor from the bullet holes to the elevator, though there were no bodies in the vicinity. Whoever it had caught, they'd gotten away.

"A trap?" Gareth asked, trying to figure out whether the person who'd triggered it had been heading deeper into the mine, or out toward the exit.

"A clumsy one," Pitorski said. "Like they wanted to keep someone from getting in."

Who had set it, though? The miners? Or the attackers?

When they reached the elevator, Pitorski cleared it

before beckoning the rest of them inside. It was made to carry entire shifts of workers deeper into the rock, and six soldiers fit comfortably inside, even with the Heralds held at the ready.

The doors shuffled open. Pitorski moved forward, while Gareth stood to the left, his partner to the right, to keep them open in case they needed to evacuate the level quickly. His feet itched to follow the Captain, to keep moving, but he stayed while the others moved on, calling clear.

And then there was silence. Sudden, alarming silence, Pitorski's voice cutting off mid-command.

Gareth exchanged a glance with his partner officer, whose eyes were wide behind his face plate. "Captain?" Gareth said. "What's your status?"

"Sir." Pitorski's voice came back sounding strained, and Gareth immediately felt himself moving away from the elevator, deeper into the room. "You'd better come. There are survivors. They're kids." Another pause. "And they're armed."

CHAPTER 9

AS SLOANE SCANNED her palm to pay for entrance to Scope's hov-train network, she couldn't help feeling a stab of annoyance at having been forced to return here. Why couldn't Damian Riddle be hanging out on an interesting planet, in a city with actual color?

It wasn't that she wanted to head back to a dangerous planet like Cal Cornum—that'd been the worst—and she wasn't asking for anything fancy. But was it wrong to hope that Fortune's guess about Damian carving out a niche in the Bone System would turn out to be right?

She might not have to fight weird mud monsters on Scope, a definite plus, but all the blandness hurt her eyes.

Sloane stepped into the train compartment, moving to stand by the clear double doors on the opposite side. The view wasn't scenic, but she wanted eyes on her surroundings. She was on edge after running from the Federation, and Striker was probably still lurking around in Torrent System, watching for her. It wasn't like she'd gone far.

A step behind her, Brighton looked dubiously at the

palm scan that'd allowed him to board the train. "Not used to paying," he said.

Sloane peered out the window, looking in vain for a flash of color. Even the birds here were brown. "We could hang you from the bottom of a drop cab again, if you want."

"No, thank you."

Ivy followed Brighton inside, and the doors slid shut behind her with a tired *whuff*. She looked rested after a couple nights on *Moneymaker*, her tattoos glowing with silvery blue light, her dark eyelids dusted with gold powder. She took hold of one of the center poles as the train glided into motion, turning the city into a blur of sandy yellow.

"I knew Damian used to have a place here," Ivy said, "but I'd been searching for weeks. I couldn't locate him."

That explained her initial presence here, at least. "For future reference," Sloane said, "that's the kind of information that would have been useful to have before I spent two days rifling through stale databases."

Ivy shrugged. "I thought it was a dead end. How did you get the exact location?"

Sloane leaned back against the doors. "My uncle's got good stuff."

Ivy raised her eyebrows and nodded, impressed. Brighton's eyebrow hike said something more like *I've seen your uncle's databases, and there's no way you found Riddle that way.*

At least he kept his mouth shut. Sloane wasn't eager to reveal her connection to the Fleet—especially since it was a tenuous one, barely worth mentioning—and she didn't want to admit she'd had to ask for help.

Brighton must have his suspicions, but maybe he thought she'd caved and looked through Oliver's things.

She'd been in Oliver's room. It was as good a cover story as any.

"Excuse me."

Sloane looked down to see a woman in a green dress who was seated on the bench to her left and staring up at her with wide eyes. And a fliptab at the ready. "You're that bounty hunter," she said.

Sloane glanced back over her shoulder. No one there. The woman was definitely talking to her. "I am?"

The woman held up her fliptab. "Will you take a picture with me?"

Sloane had gone viral a couple of times at this point, once for her embarrassing debut at that Fleet ball a couple of years ago. Now this woman was displaying a video of her crashing one of *Moneymaker*'s pods through the Fox Clan mothership's halls. Who the hell would have leaked something like that?

"That's not me," Sloane said.

The woman flipped her thumb across the screen, and a second video popped up. This one showed Sloane extracting Brighton from the fighting ring on Shard by riding the vertical drop-cab channels from the ground to the hov-train above.

It'd be really hard to pretend that wasn't her. She was even wearing the same black V-neck. Though to be fair, most of her shirts were black.

"So?" the woman said. "Will you take a picture with me?"

Sloane glanced at Ivy, who shrugged. Brighton looked like he was trying not to laugh. And there was a couple sitting on the opposite bench, who looked like they wanted to gauge her reaction so they could ask for a picture next.

"No."

The woman laughed. "Why?"

"Because it's hard to do my job when people post my location all over the galactic feeds."

"I won't post it," the woman protested. "Promise."

Right. She'd just show it to all her friends in person. Like no one in the galaxy. "Why don't I believe you?"

The woman's eyes went wide with surprise, and she lunged for Sloane, grabbing her wrist and dragging her forward toward the bench. For a second, Sloane thought she just really wanted to force the picture issue. She tried to pull back, but the woman's jaw was working in silent shock, and her grip was tight around Sloane's arm.

A blast of warm air hit Sloane's back, and she glanced over her shoulder to see that the doors she'd just been leaning on were now gaping open, the streets of Scope zipping by a dozen stories below. She stopped fighting and let the woman pull her forward, tumbling across her fan's lap and onto the floor. "Thanks," she said. "You'd better get out of here."

The couple was already up and moving toward the end of the car, and the woman in the green dress followed. Sloane could only hope they had enough sense to escape to the next car over. She picked herself up off the floor, trying to decide if she should make a run for it.

Too late. The two men who swung into the car from the roof—a good move, one to catalogue if she survived this—could not have looked more like Federation thugs if they'd been wearing *I Heart Striker* T-shirts. They were dressed in black, like they'd wanted to bring a piece of Obsidian City with them, and they both wore white Federation logos on their arms, the city's skyline surrounded by a constellation-studded map that supposedly represented the galaxy.

Brighton rushed the guy on the left, aiming a thick fist at

his nose. He was fast, but the thug was faster. Much faster than he should have been, in fact. He raised a hand so quickly it blurred, catching Brighton's punch in his palm.

And they were modded. Excellent.

The thug squeezed and pushed back, forcing Brighton further into the car, and then Sloane lost track of them as the second thug stalked toward Ivy.

Who, possibly for tattoo-related reasons, didn't look concerned. Sloane made a run for her attacker anyway, sliding across the short distance between the floor and the door to intercept him as he made for Ivy. She had half an idea of knocking him out the door, though she wasn't quite sure how to do that without flying out herself. It was one of those ideas that tended to work itself out in the doing.

Sloane's feet hit the thug in the knees, and pain jolted her ankles as the guy stayed put. Didn't even budge.

"Ivy," she said, scrambling to her feet as the guy leered down at her, "can you do that thing you do?"

"I was waiting for you to get out of the way," Ivy said. "You know, so you wouldn't die when his mods cut out."

Which would send him flying out the door, and Sloane along with him. Good thinking. Maybe it *wouldn't* have worked itself out in the doing.

Sloane was facing Henchman B—they looked too alike to give them distinguishing-characteristic nicknames in her head—when Ivy unleashed her tattoo powers, so she couldn't see the flicker-and-glow of the inlays as they worked. But she knew without looking back at Ivy that the guy's mods had failed him, because he jerked his hands up to eye level, like he needed to check his battery charge. He took a step forward, seemingly all too aware of his proximity to the gaping doors.

No one wanted to add that kind of color to Scope's sidewalks.

And then Brighton's opponent—Henchman A—went sailing into the bench to her left, his legs kicking wildly as Brighton held him down by the throat.

Sloane backed away from the door, easing her stunner out of her back pocket and aiming it at Henchman B. "Tell Striker nice try," she said.

At the far end of the car, someone cheered, and Sloane risked a glance in that direction.

Not only had the woman in the green dress stayed to watch, but so had the couple, plus a handful of other commuters. Which meant that she was now staring into the cameras of half a dozen fliptabs.

"Can I monetize this?" one of the fans asked.

"No," Sloane said. "You're in time out. All of you."

Before she could expound on what exactly she meant by that—which would require *deciding* what she meant by it—Ivy made a sound in the back of her throat that was half gasp, half gurgle, and Sloane whipped her attention back to the middle of the car in time to see her client collapse to her knees. Ivy's inlays were strobing fitfully, and as Sloane watched, the silver faded into the dull rainbows of color like the ones Oliver had worn.

By the time Sloane looked back at Henchman B, who was still framed by the door, he was grinning. "You can tell him yourself."

There weren't enough curses in enough languages. There just weren't.

Brighton's opponent pushed up from the bench suddenly and, in an unworldly show of strength, slammed Sloane's security officer back against the side of the car.

The door to the next car shuffled open, and Striker

himself entered the car, pointing some kind of handheld laser gun lazily in their direction. He must have sent his thugs ahead to scout so he could deactivate Ivy's tech. Sloane should have realized he'd be able to do that. If those bounty hunters had done it, then the CTF could, too.

Sloane dropped her weapon and took a step back, bending slightly—hands still up—to make sure Ivy was okay. But Ivy just waved at her, eyes trained on Striker.

"I don't consider myself to be a particularly fragile person," Striker said, "but I have to admit, it hurts that I didn't warrant an invitation to this party. Brighton, good to see you."

Brighton bared his teeth, but there wasn't much he could do with Henchman-A's hand vised around his neck.

"What is it with you and Fortune, heading up your own ground missions or whatever?" Sloane asked. "You obviously have the staff to handle scum like us."

Striker smiled, a slow stretch of his lips. "The Commander and I share so few similarities, but I suppose we do have that in common. I gave you a chance to surrender your fugitive. I regret that our partnership must end this way, but alas."

Sloane glared at him, pointing to the far end of the car, where the fans were watching, fliptabs still raised. She couldn't see their faces, but she hoped they regretted not evacuating when she'd told them to. "You can't just kill us. It'll be all over the feeds."

Striker shook his head. He almost looked sad. Someone watching on the feeds might think he regretted this. "You are a rogue bounty hunter and a threat to the galaxy. The feeds will celebrate."

"No, we won't," the woman in the green dress volunteered.

Maybe he looked more like a psycho murderer, after all. Striker's next move would be to murder all the spectators and blame it on Sloane, but she wasn't sure how to warn the woman that it was a distinct possibility.

"It wasn't a question," Striker said.

"Then what was it?" Sloane was fully aware that she was stalling at this point, but she supposed she couldn't be blamed for wanting to keep her organs intact. "A command? I don't think it works like that."

Striker rolled his eyes. "I officially rescind my job offer, Ms. Tarnish. Goodbye."

And then a pair of boots swung through the open doors and directly into the side of Striker's face, knocking him to the floor.

The person who belonged to the boots swung back, a thick twist of rope clasped in his hands, and landed on his feet. He grinned. "A perfect hit."

Sloane barely had time to process this before Henchman A lunged for the newcomer. But he had to free Brighton in the process, and though Brighton might not be modded, he was quick; in a moment, he'd slammed Henchman A's head into the wall, hard, and the man slumped to the floor.

Henchman B took one look at his boss and his friend and, clearly deciding to cut his losses, raised his hands in the air.

The newcomer had on worn brown boots that reached nearly to his knees, and a long leather duster that had absolutely seen better days. He had a mop of suspiciously mussed red-brown hair, as if he'd arranged it to look exactly as messy as he wanted. As far as Sloane could tell, the rope in his hands appeared to be attached to the roof of the still-moving train.

And he was familiar. Very familiar.

"Damian Riddle," Sloane said. "You look exactly like your comics."

Damian pressed his hand flat against his chest. "That might be the nicest thing anyone's ever said to me." He freed a strand of rope from the tangle and tossed it to her, then did the same for Ivy and Brighton. "Now let's get the fuck out of here, shall we?"

CHAPTER 10

THE TEENAGE GIRL wasn't just armed; she was gripping a mid-sized hand cannon. Those things were heavy, and the barrel ran nearly the length of her arm, but she had it leveled directly at Pitorski's face. There wasn't much armor in the world that could protect against a hand-cannon blast, not at this range, and almost any helmet visor would shatter in the face of a point-blank shot.

Pitorski was facing the girl with her hands in the air, her own weapon already on the floor at her feet. The other three soldiers did the same, though they stood a few paces closer to the elevator doors.

The girl was thin, with streaks of dirt running down her face, a strip of cloth tying her dark hair back, though the frizzy strands were doing their best to escape her efforts. She held the cannon awkwardly, and Gareth could see that she'd twisted the straps around her forearm in such a way that a shot from the gun would land her with a spiderweb of fractures up her arm. The strap was meant to brace against kickback—not insignificant, with a hand cannon—but not when it was knotted like that.

Gareth raised his own hands slowly, noting the way his partner did the same in his peripheral vision. He'd been in enough combat situations to recognize the face of someone who was backed into a corner and absolutely would pull the trigger. This girl had the guts to stare down a squad of Fleet soldiers in full armor, her lips peeled away from her teeth, brow crunched in concentration, and though her hands were shaking, the glint in her eyes said she'd do what needed to be done.

The only wonder was that she hadn't taken a shot yet.

Gareth risked a glance over the girl's shoulder, trying to take in their surroundings while also keeping an eye on that trigger finger. He hoped she would give him a minute to think before she decided to start shooting.

They were standing in a kind of cavern, with a trio of old mine cars abandoned against the right wall and a line of dusty storage lockers at the far end. One of the lockers had a half-ripped poster taped up on the door, a ragged sliver of color in an otherwise gray room. Like the cafeteria, the walls and floor were made of rock. A storage room, maybe.

Huddled in the corner, between the lockers and the wall, were a dozen more children. One of them, another teenager, sat at the front with her back to the rest of the kids, like she was the last line of defense should her friend with the gun fail. But she had a bloody bandage tied to her leg, and Gareth wasn't sure how long she'd last.

Anger surged into his chest—who could have done this? And to *children?*—and he breathed through it. Someone needed to speak, before this situation careened out of control. "We're not here to hurt you," he said gently.

A squad of armor-encased soldiers facing a huddling group of children. It was too little, too...too like something a villain might say in an entertainment vid. It sounded false, even to his ears.

The girl with the gun laughed, a mirthless, hysterical burst of sound. "Then go," she said. "We don't need you."

Gareth let his gaze skip behind her, deliberately this time. "Your friend is injured. She needs help, and we have medical supplies. My name is—"

"I know who you are." The girl licked her lips, which were dry and cracked. How long had it been since these kids had eaten? Or had anything to drink? "I might live out in a nowhere zone, but I do see the feeds."

He'd been known to turn up in them from time to time. "All right."

The girl jerked the gun. Pitorski flinched. "It was your traps that shot up her leg," the girl said. "Why would you want to heal it? Just so you can blow it up again?"

Gareth's head swam with confusion, his thoughts heavy and slow. The other girl must have been the one to set off that trap in the corridor. Had she been trying to find a way out? She was lucky to be alive.

"We only just arrived," Gareth said. "We couldn't have set any traps. And we wouldn't, in any case."

The girl looked back at him, her eyes a mixture of defiance and terror. If it came down to it, the soldiers could disarm her; she'd get a shot off, maybe hurt or even kill one of them, but they'd overpower her. She had to know that.

But Gareth didn't want anyone to get hurt. And he didn't want to drag these kids away from here against their will. He wanted to help.

The way she was looking at him, though, the girl wasn't buying it. "I might be a mine brat, but I know a Fleet corvette when I see one," she said. "I saw the ships come in. I was helping my dad on the docks."

She finished the sentence with a half-sob that told him she knew exactly what had become of her dad. Gareth wanted to take whoever'd done this and shove their face into the wall.

"A Fleet corvette," he repeated. "Which one? Was it called the *Dirk*?"

She shrugged, a shivering rattle of her thin shoulders. "I didn't see the names. There were two of them, though."

"And the soldiers?" he asked. "Did you see them?"

She shrugged and wiped the back of her free hand across her nose, then dropped it quickly, as though realizing suddenly that it might give away her tears. "They had on armor. Not like yours, but close enough."

Pitorski exchanged a glance with the soldier beside her, and Gareth felt like he could read her thoughts. A Fleet corvette couldn't have done this, *wouldn't* have. Not under his command. Pitorski knew that.

And yet, this girl had *seen* the ships. Fleet ships showed up on the feeds often enough to be recognized. She hadn't just said they were Fleet ships; she knew they were corvettes, specifically.

Maybe the *Dirk* and the *Hunter* hadn't gone missing at all. Maybe they'd gone rogue.

Gareth swallowed the bile that rose in his throat at the thought. Maybe he really had done this, after all. But he wouldn't get any answers with a gun in his face, or with these children still in danger.

The kids were all breathing comfortably in here, so Gareth raised his face plate, palms still spread open at his shoulders, and stepped up to stand right next to Pitorski. He half expected her to object, in which case he'd have a tough choice to make here—he didn't want to break his promise to her about her command, but this had gone beyond a routine ground sweep—but she didn't say anything.

"What's your name?" he asked the girl.

She glanced behind her, toward her friend, as if looking for some indication of what she should do. But the injured girl's attention was on the younger kids. He could almost see her calculating, trying to figure out how she'd get them out of here if his soldiers decided to attack.

It made his heart want to crack in half.

From here, he might be able to knock the cannon out of the girl's hand, might slice through the wrist cords with his suit's tools before she could reach the trigger. Might. But he stayed where he was, waiting until she returned her attention to him.

She met his gaze, her eyes dark and terrified. "Beth," she said.

Gareth risked a half step forward, pointing to his open face plate. "I'm trusting you, Beth. And you can trust me, too. We didn't send those ships here, but we'd very much like to find out who did. You might be able to help us."

Her lip trembled. "How?"

"You're witnesses." He kept his voice calm and low, as easy and gentle as he could manage. "You can tell us everything you recall about the ships, and about the attackers."

She gave her head a shake, like she was trying to dislodge a fly. Or his appearance of kindness. "They were soldiers. Like you."

"Soldiers, maybe," Gareth said. "But *not* like us. I promise you that. I want to know who did this so I can stop them. Do you believe me?"

Beth's hand tightened around the handle of the gun, and Pitorski drew in a breath like she was about to watch her Commander die. But then Beth dropped her hand to her side, releasing the gun like it was poison. The cords kept it dangling from her wrist, the barrel twisting dangerously.

Pitorski was already moving, dropping to her knees to cut the cords and retrieve the gun. Quick on her feet, that one. Maybe primed for a promotion before too long.

"Yeah," Beth said, her head bent like someone who'd lost a fight. "Maybe."

"Okay. It's a deal." Gareth tugged off his glove and extended his hand, waiting for Beth to take it.

She squinted up into his face, looked down at his hand like it was some kind of trick, then slid her fingers into his. She gave them a brief squeeze before letting go, as if she expected him to grab her and haul her away against her will after all. "Deal."

In a day full of misery, they'd managed to do something right. He'd take the win.

Pitorski's visor was still snapped on tight, and her voice piped into his ear through the helmet comm. "Sir, we need to clear a safe path before we extract the kids."

Gareth nodded, still trying to keep a calm expression on his face for Beth's sake. He understood what the Captain was trying to say; they couldn't walk the kids back through the massacre, nor could they risk an alternate route that might be full of traps.

"Go ahead," he said. "I'll stay here, if that's all right with you."

Pitorski gestured for the others to follow her, leaving one guard behind to keep an eye on the door.

Gareth watched while Beth went to the kids, doing his best to appear solid and reliable—if he could even lay claim to those qualities anymore—while giving her space to gather them. She'd been leading them, and they trusted her. No need to hover.

While he waited, he composed a brief update to Lager and sent it off via his eye screen, hoping the Lieutenant might miraculously be somewhere in-Current where he could send off a brief reply. It was a shame that his friend was off ship at the moment; Lager would be the perfect person to calm these terrified kids, with his disarming smile and his charm. He probably even knew a magic trick or two. Maybe he could teach one to Gareth.

But Lager didn't respond. Too far off for direct communication, then. Gareth messaged *Sabre* asking for counselors to meet them at the bay when they returned, with anyone who had experience with kids at the front. Stills confirmed the order, and the channel went quiet again.

He waited a minute, and then another, watching while Beth helped the younger kids into jackets and wiped grit off their faces with her sleeve. These poor kids had been through hell. He hoped the Fleet could help them. Find someone to take them in.

He couldn't believe those Fleet ships had gone rogue. He outright *refused* to believe it. His people believed in their mission. If that weren't enough, Captain West's spies watched the Fleet as carefully as they watched the rest of the galaxy, and they'd have picked up rumors of mutiny.

No, the ships hadn't gone rogue. Gareth believed in his people. In a fit of wild optimism—and, he had to admit, a dash of ill-advised recklessness—he dashed off a sentence to Alisa March.

I hope we can speak again soon.

She might still be in-Current. She might be willing to respond. She might be willing to listen, as she always had been before.

It was too short, not nearly equal to the circumstances. He wasn't sure what he expected her to say in response. 'Of course, you're right, let me drop my absolute certainty that you're a treasonous bastard and listen to your side of the story'? Not too likely.

Olton Moon was one thing, but what additional evidence had Osmond Clay laid before Alisa—what atrocities had he blamed on Gareth—that could convince her to turn against him like this? And not just Alisa, but half the Commission? There had to be more than she was saying.

Gareth's stomach twisted, thinking of the dead miners, of the destroyed water hauler. If Fleet corvettes had done this, perhaps he'd given her some very compelling evidence indeed.

Pitorski returned, ready to guide the kids safely back to *Sabre*.

Alisa never responded.

CHAPTER 11

AS SLOANE FELL out of the moving car with Damian Riddle's rope secured to the back of her belt, it occurred to her that it might not be the best policy to trust a complete stranger to drop her safely from the inside of a multi-story hov-train. The fact that Damian himself was falling at the same rate, by way of the same mechanism, wasn't as much of a comfort as it perhaps might have been.

Especially when he didn't slow as they neared the ground.

"Are we going to die?" Sloane yelled.

Damian's answering grin was wild with joy. "Not today, bounty hunter."

The bleached landscape of the city was approaching far faster than Sloane would have preferred. She could hear Brighton calling out a stream of curses behind her, but she couldn't see her security officer's face.

She doubted he'd ever step back on a hov-train again, assuming they all survived this.

Damian shot ahead of her like an arrow, arms raised over his head, the wind lifting his long coat into a flutter around his waist as he aimed his legs for the street. He was a beat ahead of her, heels pointed at what looked to Sloane like a solid square of sidewalk, distinguished from the rest of the block only by the fact that it was surrounded by white construction markers.

So she'd get to see the pirate's legs shatter before she succumbed to the same fate. No problem.

She just barely had time to hear Damian whoop before his feet disappeared straight into the pavement.

Sloane bit back a curse as her feet sank into the ground behind him.

"Drop the rope!" Damian yelled, and she did. Her ass hit something hard and kept going as a plasteel slide caught her fall and whirled her down below ground level.

A blink of sliding darkness, punctuated by Brighton's continued stream of curses and Damian's gleeful cackles, and then Sloane was flying off the end of the slide. She landed on a mat, the cushion absorbing her fall, and rolled forward just in time for Brighton and Ivy to come hurtling down behind her.

Heart skittering in her chest, Sloane picked herself up off the floor, staggering slightly while also glaring at Damian with what she hoped was a terrifying look of fury. "Why couldn't you just say 'The pavement's a hologram, we're not going to die'?"

He was grinning at her like she was an angry kitten. She was half tempted to stun him in the hip just to punish him. "Can't give away the game, now, can I?"

Damian swiveled and offered Ivy his hand. She ignored him, getting to her feet on her own. Damian gave her a short bow, then strode off the mats. "This way."

Brighton was the last to rise. He gave his shoulders a shake and lifted an eyebrow at Sloane. "I resign," he said.

Sloane patted him on the arm. "Okay. Hope Halorin System doesn't find you."

Brighton cringed, then looked around. "What is this place?"

Sloane hadn't bothered to survey their surroundings yet. She did so now, turning a slow circle to take in Damian's underground world.

Scope apparently did have some color. It was all just...underground.

Murals splashed across the wide-set corridor, bright abstract scenes full of reds, oranges, and blues. They filled every corner, coating the ceiling and the concrete beneath their feet. No beige in sight. The people who strode through halls wore the most ostentatious clothing she'd ever seen, puffed out pants and layered dresses that combined eye-searingly bright colors, sunshine yellows wedged in with tomato reds, and a shade of blue that reminded her of a swimming pool.

Music blasted from several spots at once, some of it coming and going with one of the passersby, some remaining steady. As she watched, a pair of hov-tilers wove through the crowd with ease, knees bent for balance, their feet zooming several inches off the ground. They were laughing, and she got the distinct impression that this was a race.

If she tried to do that, she'd bang her head on the ceiling for sure.

"What is this place?" she said.

Damian was waiting patiently a few paces down the corridor, propped against the wall with his hands in his pockets. "Welcome to Scope Underground," he said. "Are you done gaping yet?"

She wasn't, but she moved to join him anyway, with

Brighton and Ivy a step behind. Damian flowed away from the wall with a casual kind of grace and started into the crowd, apparently trusting her to follow. He waved to a woman with a beverage cart, and she smiled at him like he was her grandson before handing him a lime-green drink. Sloane didn't see any money change hands, didn't catch the scan of Damian's palm, only the solemn nod he gave her as he lifted the drink to his mouth. Who were these people? And who was Damian?

The floor sloped downward as they walked, widening into an area where screens dotted the walls at varying intervals. Mostly, they displayed dance videos and snippets of cartoons she'd watched as a kid, but here and there a news item filtered into her vision.

She slowed when she caught sight of Osmond Clay, his face dominating an entire corner. Cappel System's weaselly-looking governor wore robes that hung around his wrists like gaping mouths as he held forth on the Fleet Advisory Commission. "The upcoming summit in Cappel System represents a new horizon for the Fleet," he was saying, his voice mixing with the sound effects from the cartoons playing on the next screen over. "It will usher forth an age of trust between the galaxy and its military partners."

She hadn't realized Clay was so prominent in the FAC. Or that he was such an obvious ass. Not that she paid much attention to these things. Didn't Fortune suspect the guy of trying to have him assassinated, though? Seemed odd that he wouldn't have mentioned that Clay also headed up the Commission.

Sloane realized Damian was waiting for her again, and she picked up the pace, even as Ivy drifted into step beside her. Her client's eyes were pinned to Damian's back, and she was chewing her bottom lip like she was rehearsing exactly what she planned to say to him.

"You acted like Damian Riddle was a stranger to you," Sloane said.

Ivy squared her shoulders. "Yes, well. It's embarrassing."

"What? You dated him or something?" She couldn't quite picture the two together, but she supposed that stranger opposites had attracted. For some reason, that thought brought Fortune to mind, but she dismissed him quickly from her mind.

The point was, she wasn't about to shame Ivy, or anyone else, for a mistaken romantic encounter or two.

"No," Ivy said. "he's sort of my stepbrother."

Damian didn't look like the kind of person who had stepsisters. He looked like the kind of person who had bartenders, rusted out spy bots, and frequent-customer cards at a variety of brothels.

But then, there *had* been the old woman with the smoothie.

"Again," Sloane said, "that's the kind of information that would have been helpful *before* I started looking for him."

Ivy sighed. "Yeah, sorry."

Sloane wondered how other hunters got the full information, and crucial details, out of their clients. She suspected that no one lied to Octo-Girl, or her muscled-up partner.

Then again, maybe those guys didn't need the whole story in order to do their jobs.

"Does that mean you're related to Archimedes Sol?" Sloane asked. "Because I really am sorry I tried to rob him that time. Trust me, I'm pretty sure he won that round. And several more after that."

That'd been one of her first jobs. And badly botched, despite Oliver's supposed knowledge of criminal enterprises.

Ivy shrugged. "He *was* my stepfather, before he decided to leave the Interplanetary Dwellers to make his fortune."

Right. Good to know. Did that mean Damian had tattoos like Ivy's? Sloane hadn't seen any, but Damian had hardly stopped moving since he'd come crashing into that train car, so it was tough to tell.

Damian turned a corner—the first one Sloane had seen down here—and started down a narrow set of stone steps. Just as Sloane was beginning to wonder whether he planned to lock them in some convoluted dungeon, he stopped, fished an old-fashioned key out of his pocket, and slid it into a thick wooden door.

"This is home," he said.

When Fortune had said Damian kept a place on Scope, Sloane had pictured a beige-painted apartment set inside a beige-sided building on Scope's surface. This place looked like the kind of hole a sizable rodent might claim in the side of a hill. She wouldn't be surprised to walk in and find that Damian had amassed a collection of acorns inside.

A few steps through a narrow passage, though, and Sloane had to revise her expectations. Because Damian's rodent hole was *enormous*.

He ushered them into a wide, round room, where staircases crisscrossed the shelf-lined walls, leading up to various doors and other hallways. The shelves were packed with junk, item after item that defied categorization: a pale statue with a milk-white drape of cloth tossed over the good bits; a goblet that might have been crystal, with a crack of shining silver running through the stem; a stack of bound books, the pages crumpled and yellow; and wood-sided crates with tufts of packing straw peeking through the slats, dozens of them, stacked haphazardly around the edges of the room.

And there were clocks. *Hundreds* of clocks. They filled the room with ticks and whirs, chimes and cheeps, plus the smell of grease and fresh-cut wood. They were shaped like spaceships, like houses, like birds and trees and, in one case, an overstuffed chair. Damian had them tucked between the rest of his treasure—or junk; she couldn't quite tell—like knickknacks, like they were the main attraction, and the rest of it was just detritus.

"Why clocks?" Sloane asked.

Damian shed his coat and dropped it across the back of a wooden chair. "Clocks. They fascinate me. In a galaxy where time is practically irrelevant, everyone running on the light of different stars, they're just..." He waved a hand at the shelves, as if searching for a word that Sloane was ninety-nine percent sure he already knew he was going to say. "Quaint," he finished.

She had to admit that she didn't have a good read on this guy yet. Still, she'd have bet a not-insignificant number of tokens that there were secrets to be found in some of those clocks.

"Okay," Sloane said. "Why did you help us on the train? Did you know Ivy was with us?"

Damian settled himself at the foot of one of the staircases, stretching his legs out long, his arms spread out at his sides. He looked like he might fall asleep. "Stars, no," he said. "No offense, Ives, but I would've avoided you." He shook an index finger in her direction, though he paired it with a lazy smile. "I know all about that little bounty you've posted."

"Silly me," Ivy said.

"No, it wasn't about Ivy," Damian said, dropping his hand back to the step. "I admit that I enjoy the occasional swashbuckling moment. I saw trouble, and, well, there you have it."

Damian pointed to the shelf above his head, where a pair of comic-book posters were pasted on the wall between a rolled-up mat and a clock shaped like a flower. Again, Sloane wondered if he'd written the things himself.

"So you're a hero," she said.

"If you like. Also, and I cannot emphasize this enough, I hate the Cosmic Trade Federation. They are always up in my business."

Sloane glanced around at the treasures-slash-junk. If Damian wasn't some kind of smuggler, she'd eat her own stunner. "I bet they are," she said.

"I'd offer you refreshments," Damian said, "but I don't have any. I hope you know I won't let you turn me in to the CTF."

He said it casually, but there was a glint in his eye that said the relaxed demeanor and the lazy charm were a front for something dangerous. Something sharp.

"But then," he said, his tone still easy, "they did seem to be after *you,* so I suppose that's not on the itinerary. What *is* your plan, if I may be so bold?"

Ivy rolled her eyes, like she wanted to punch her sort-of-stepbrother in the mouth just to get a break from that smile of his. Brighton had stationed himself by the door, as if he expected a break-in at any moment.

Sloane crossed the room and sat down in the chair where Damian had slung his coat. "Ivy says she wants to take you to the Interplanetary Dwellers."

"I really do," Ivy said.

Damian blinked, cocking his head to the side. He looked, Sloane thought, like a curious sort of bird. "Interesting," he murmured.

"I guess they're still mad about some heist you tried to pull off," she said.

Damian pointed his finger at her, but his smile didn't slip. He wore a thick golden band on his right ring finger, with a seal that swelled over most of his bottom finger joint, though Sloane couldn't make out the stamp on it.

"Not tried," he corrected. "Succeeded in. Succeeded in pulling off."

"My mistake," Sloane said, as if the slip hadn't been intentional. She'd wanted to see what his response would be, and she suspected he knew it.

Damian tapped his bottom lip with his finger, though Sloane was pretty sure it was another affectation, another part of the ongoing Damian Riddle show. He knew what he wanted from them, likely had known since before he'd extracted them from that train. "All right," he said. "I accept."

Sloane frowned, not sure she'd heard him correctly. "What?"

"I'll go," Damian said. "I'll be your prisoner. I've been wanting to get another crack at the Interplanetary Dwellers for years."

Ivy moved closer, eyes scanning the room as if she expected one of the clocks to attack. "You do understand you'd be a *real* prisoner. That we'll leave you there and they'll lock you up. Put you on trial."

Damian gave his hand a wave, as though flicking her words away. "Yes, yes. Leave that to me. No worries at all. Now, does your ship need supplies? Any other stops before we leave Scope?"

"No," Sloane said, "we're good."

"Do you have cookies?"

Sloane frowned. "I...what?"

"All of my contracts include the provision of baked goods," Damian said. "Specifically, cookies."

"I have cookies," Brighton said.

"Excellent." Damian unfolded himself from the steps in a matter of seconds, then whipped his coat off the back of Sloane's chair. "Let's go."

CHAPTER 12

THE MESSAGE from Lager came in while Gareth was helping the kids settle in on *Sabre*.

Nothing notable yet, Lager's note read, *but I assumed you wouldn't want to miss this*.

He'd attached a video, but it wasn't marked urgent, so Gareth set it aside. The counselors had suggested they keep the kids together, and he'd spent the first few hours after their evacuation in one of the mess halls, helping to shove tables aside, arrange cots, and assemble a meal for them. A few soldiers went digging through supplies for toys to occupy the younger kids, while ground teams combed the asteroid inch by inch, searching for clues.

So far, they'd only found bodies.

By the time the counselors convinced him to leave the hall—now a makeshift dormitory—with assurances that they had everything well in hand, Gareth's head was thrumming with exhaustion and grief, and it wasn't until he'd showered and returned to his cabin that he remembered Lager's message, and the unwatched video.

Long day. Very long. Gareth sat down at his desk—just

a strip of metal that'd been bolted to the wall, with a metal chair to match it—and opened the file, not quite knowing what to expect.

The hov-train in the video might have been anywhere in the galaxy; their interiors were fairly standard. But even though the landscape blurred by too quickly for him to make out the exact location, he knew the train had to be on Scope. Because Sloane Tarnish was front and center, and she was doing her best to knock a very large Federation employee out of the open doors.

Why the train doors were open while the train was careening above the city, well, that was anyone's guess. It was Sloane, which meant anything was possible.

Someone had taken the video from the far end of the car, and their hand was shaking badly—no surprise there—but the picture was clear enough. Gareth watched, heart in his throat, as Striker swaggered into the shot. The train was humming too loudly for him to hear what the Federation coordinator was saying, but Gareth could imagine it well enough. Threats, taunts, and more threats. Striker was nothing if not predictable, at least in that respect.

The video jolted, and then a man in a long coat was swinging into the car and planting his boots directly in Striker's face.

Damian Riddle. Dramatic entrances might as well be the man's middle name. While Gareth watched, Damian handed Sloane a rope, and they were jumping out of the still-moving car together. Brighton Walsh followed, along with a woman Gareth didn't recognize.

The video ended, and Gareth realized he was smiling. It'd been the worst kind of day, the kind that made him want to bury his head in his hand and weep. But seeing her like that...it eased something in him, something he hadn't quite realized was hurting. Like a balm that soaked into the skin. Healing.

Before he quite knew what he intended, Gareth was initiating a direct call to her. She was likely still on Scope, so he'd have to leave a message. He'd take it.

But she must have been in-Current, because only a few seconds passed before she accepted the contact request.

"Starting a revolution, are you?" Gareth said.

"Don't lecture me, Fortune," she replied, but she sounded like she was smiling. At least, he wanted to picture her that way. He wanted to imagine that she knew exactly what he meant.

He wanted to imagine them on the same side.

"On the contrary," he said. "I liked it. Quite the exit. You met Damian, I see."

She hesitated, and he found himself pretending he could listen to the distance between them, all the waves and frequencies crowding the vacuum that separated the two ships. He tapped his fingers on the desk, trying to ground himself in the here and now. The problem was, he wasn't sure he *wanted* to stay in the here and now.

"You sound sad," she said.

She could hear that in his voice? Gareth sat back in the chair, trying to replay what he'd said in his mind. How could she tell?

"Yes, well," he said. "Tough day."

"You headed out to this FAC summit thing?"

"I'm not invited." He said it without thinking, without considering that she was only making conversation. She didn't need to know the ins and outs of the summit, of Fleet politics, and he'd called to...why *had* he called? To make sure she was safe? It hardly seemed necessary after that exit.

In reality, he'd called because he wanted to hear her voice. It was as simple as that.

"Fortune." Sloane sounded disbelieving, or maybe like she was scolding him, though that couldn't be right. "You need to go to the meeting. I saw that overdressed assassin on the feeds today, yammering about a new Galaxy and a new world for the Commission and the Fleet. He's trying to undermine you."

"A fact of which I'm well aware."

"So you need to go."

It was surprising that she cared so vehemently about what Osmond Clay was doing. The man was a tumor, sure enough, but Gareth's attendance at some trumped-up meeting in Cappel wouldn't change that. It wouldn't change Alisa's mind, or anyone else's. There were more pressing matters to deal with. Real problems.

The line was quiet for a moment, the miles stretching between them like taffy. Distance was a malleable thing. She was far away, but she was close, too. He'd never quite understood the Currents, never quite grasped how the technology allowed for this...bending, this play with space and time. In this moment, he wished he did.

"They're up to something," Sloane said. "You do realize this."

Sloane was opinionated; that, he knew. But he wouldn't have expected her to side so vehemently against Clay. And he certainly wouldn't have expected her to echo Alisa's call for him to make an appearance at this summit. What had Alisa said? Clay was passing around a story, something about Gareth refusing to attend, when in truth he was withholding the information Gareth would need to get there.

Cappel was an insular System, relying on its own resources. They allowed no outsiders to enter their territory, not even vendors, and Fleet intelligence hadn't ever managed to get a foothold there. If Clay wanted Gareth in attendance, he'd need to send exact information about how to enter the System, as he'd have done for the members of the FAC.

Of course, Gareth hadn't pursued that information, either, or requested it. But to say he'd outright refused to attend? That was a lie.

So yes, he knew Clay was up to something. It was difficult to ignore.

Gareth sighed. "I've been...distracted." He let the silence stretch for another moment. When she didn't say anything, he added, "Well, I'm glad you're all right."

"I'm always all right."

"I'm still glad."

"It's your job, yeah?"

Was it? He worked to keep people safe, sure, but checking in on unorthodox bounty hunters was not a typical item on his to-do list.

Before he could form a response, she said, "I'll catch you later, Fortune."

And then the connection was gone, a lost band of frequency in a galaxy that felt, suddenly, like it was far too big.

Why had Lager sent the vid in the first place? Gareth hardly needed to watch as Sloane threw herself head-first into some new adventure. She'd *always* be on a new adventure, at least until she found her uncle—or until her father managed to wrench her back to the safety of the Center Systems. Good luck to him with that; knowing Sloane, she'd manage to elude him forever.

She and Damian would make a good team, come to think of it. The thought hit his brain and stuck there like a splinter, far more irritating than it should have been. He wanted her to have strong allies, didn't he? Damian was as good as any. If he could be trusted to stay an ally, which was never a guarantee.

Gareth was preparing for a sleepless shift on his bunk, another night counting the bolts in the ceiling, when a notification from Stills flickered across his eye screen.

Sorry to interrupt your off-shift, sir, the message read, *but Lieutenant Lager's cube ship just went dark. We can't raise them.*

Gareth had never dressed more quickly in his life, a lump of fear hot in the back of his throat. He bolted up to the bridge, where several members of navigation and communication were clustered around Stills' console, discussing its contents with barely concealed panic.

Lager would have had the maps up on the viewport by now, but without him here, Gareth had to ask for them. He worked hard to keep his voice calm as he bypassed the bridge, clattering down the stairs to join the huddle of officers and get a look at the data with his own eyes.

"The ship vanished this morning, ship time," Stills said, without taking her eyes off the screen. "We just got the updated location stats."

The stats could take half a day to refresh, sometimes, when a ship was halfway across the galaxy. But Gareth shook his head. "That's impossible. Lager sent me a message just a few hours ago."

Stills licked her lips, glancing up at the map on the viewport. "May I see it, sir?"

Gareth handed his fliptab to her, and she scrolled through to the message information without scanning its contents. "This is more recent," she said, sounding surprised. She swiveled back to her console, keeping his fliptab next to her on the console. She tapped in some coordinates, then beckoned another officer closer. He looked back and forth between the two screens, then nodded.

"This is good, sir," Stills said. "It gives a more recent update."

"And?"

"Lager sent this from the border of Cappel System."

Gareth pressed his palms into his hips, tipping his head back to stare up at the angry red spot on the viewport that represented his friend's missing ship. "Why would Lager send a message from the border of Cappel claiming he had no updates?"

And why would he have included a video from the feeds, of all things, rather than an SOS?

"Maybe he didn't know he'd gone dark," Stills said. "Maybe they flew into a trap."

Or maybe it'd been a warning. A last signal, seemingly harmless to anyone who dug into communications. He could see Lager pulling a trick like that.

Gareth wished he were standing back up on the bridge's upper level, that he could squeeze the metal rail until his knuckles whitened. "All right," he said. "Redirect *Katana* to finish the investigation out here. We'll transfer the kids and the counselors to her before we head out."

There'd be plenty of time to make the summit, if *Katana* burned hard to get here now. He needed to get to Cappel, but there was no way he'd bring those children anywhere near a place where Fleet ships were disappearing.

"Yes, sir," Stills said, already typing. "Where is *Sabre* headed?"

Gareth made himself relax his hands. Sloane's disbelieving tone echoed in his ears. "We're going to Cappel. We've got a fancy meeting to crash."

CHAPTER 13

AS FAR AS Sloane could tell, Alex had hardly set foot in her laboratory since dismantling the wormhole generator that'd represented her life's work—until it'd threatened to implode the universe. Or something like that. Sloane was fuzzy on the details. But the room had sat empty since then, pretty much, as if Alex could make the place disappear by refusing to acknowledge its existence. Felt like denial to Sloane, but she was hardly one to give meaningful life advice, so mostly she didn't try.

As soon as Sloane had returned from Scope with Damian, Brighton, and Ivy—and her glitched-out inlays—Alex had ushered the former Interplanetary Dweller into her lab like it was the most natural thing in the world.

Now, she had Ivy seated on the same table where the almost-disastrous invention had previously stood, and she was prodding at the woman's tattooed inlays with some instrument Sloane didn't recognize. She looked inappropriately giddy that the inlays had glitched—thanks to Striker's device—making it acceptable for her to study them up close.

To Sloane's surprise, Hilda had also joined them in the

lab. With *Moneymaker* traveling in-Current again, she could relax her schedule a bit. Let the autopilot take over. Though Sloane would have expected her to play some games with her parakeet, or place bets on an upcoming race. Whatever she did in her off time.

But Hilda had stationed herself in the door of the lab, and was currently engaged in staring at Ivy, brow furrowed, lips rolled so far between her teeth that they'd almost disappeared. She looked like a parent whose kid had returned at dawn with the class rebel. Sloane had hoped she might relax her suspicion after that first meeting with Ivy. Apparently not.

Sloane had settled herself up on the nearest counter and folded her hands in her lap to keep herself from fiddling with important equipment. She figured she should stay in here, just in case those murderous glances turned into punches at some point. Though what she'd be able to do if that did happen, she wasn't sure.

"Ivy should be in med bay with you examining her," Alex said, as if she wasn't the one who'd dragged Ivy in here and started yanking equipment off shelves. "You're the one who studied healer tech. Or she should be with Brighton. He's the hacker."

Denial. Definitely denial. "I saw the way you looked at the inlays when Ivy told us about them," Sloane said. "I thought I was going to have to stop you from drooling on her arm."

Ivy raised an eyebrow in a perfect arch. She'd become marginally less mysterious since she'd first accosted Sloane in that club on Federation, but her ability to separate her eyebrows like that gave her an extra notch in the enigmatic column.

"I'm an astrophysicist. Not..." Alex waved her fingers, as though searching for a word. "Whatever this is."

"Do I really need to point out that you were waiting for us on the other side of the gangplank when we got back from Scope? I'm pretty sure you'd have bitten me if I'd tried to take her to the infirmary."

Alex wrinkled her nose. "Only because I knew you'd force me to study the inlays, so I thought I'd save you the trouble."

"So you *were* ready to bite, then."

Alex sniffed. "Of course."

Sloane could never tell if the scientist was joking.

Ivy crossed her legs, like she was attending a ballet rather than submitting to an unwilling examination. Unwilling on the doctor's part, that was. "The inlays rely on astrophysics to work," she said. "I don't know the specifics, but I know they relay data from distant stars, or..." She shook her head. "I'm sorry. It's not my area of expertise. You'll have to ask the Interplanetary Dwellers about it when we get there, though I don't know how much they'll say. All I know is that I can use the inlays to locate their station. If we get them working again."

Alex snatched Ivy's arm back up, simultaneously reaching for a rack of tools that was gathering dust at the far end of the table. "Why didn't you say so? That requires a whole different set of instruments."

Ivy glanced at Sloane. "She's difficult to please."

"You have no idea," Sloane said. But it took a concerted effort to keep her expression neutral, because Alex hadn't shown that much interest in anything since the wormhole incident. Aside from the fiery passion she'd displayed with regards to soaking dishes.

"Fun fact!" BRO said. Hilda rolled her eyes in anticipation of whatever nonsense the AI was about to start spouting. "Actually, I don't have a fun fact about astrophysics, or Interplanetary Dwellers! I just wanted to be included!"

"Thanks, BRO," Sloane said. "You're always included."

"Hurray!"

Sloane wondered, idly, if BRO might be able to tell her where Fortune had been when he'd called her. She hadn't given any thought to the witnesses who'd been on the hovtrain, and it hadn't crossed her mind that videos would be hitting the feeds. Though considering the fan's hopeful smile as she'd asked to take a photo with Sloane, she should have.

Fortune had seen the vid, and he'd wanted to talk to her. But his voice had sounded ragged. Heavy. Oh, the man was always serious; there was no denying that. But when he'd called, he'd sounded worse than serious. He'd sounded like he was grieving. What kind of trouble had he gotten himself into?

Sloane was still considering whether BRO could tell her anything about his whereabouts when *Moneymaker* shuddered, then lurched. Hard.

Sloane slid across the counter, her shoulder smashing into a metal cabinet at the end before she righted herself. Alex had braced her body against the table, her hands still locked around Ivy's wrists to keep her from falling.

By the time Sloane scrambled down from the counter and ran for the doorway, Hilda was already out of it, braid swinging as she bolted past the cabins and up the spiral staircase that led through the kitchen to the pilot's deck.

The view awaiting them was...unexpected.

The blue-green walls of the Current had vanished, replaced by the utter stillness of interstellar space.

That was not a thing that happened. Ever.

And someone was waiting for them. Some*thing*.

The ship—station? she couldn't quite peg it as either—sat motionless in the void, its size impossible to determine without the visual context of a planet or another ship to compare it to. It was shaped like a wide, flat disk, with a hull the color of burnished brass. It looked as if someone had tossed a fat coin into the abyss, perhaps accompanied by a very strange wish.

"Did they just yank us out of the Current?" Sloane asked as she dropped into the co-pilot's seat. She didn't see a System star, or any planets. Nothing but distant stars, shining clear and bright.

Hilda sucked her cheeks between her teeth and bit down, hard. "Yes."

"Fun fact!" BRO said. "That's not possible!"

Before Sloane could open communications or decide what to say to these people—she figured they might as well assume they were dealing with people, until proven otherwise—a regal-toned voice reverberated through the pilot's deck.

"Greetings, *Moneymaker*," the female-sounding voice said. "We would like to invite you to join the Interplanetary Dwellers for a meeting aboard the Atom."

The Atom. Looked more like a pancake than a building block of the universe, but fine. "Is that a ship, or a station?" Sloane asked.

"It is neither. It is both."

Oh, how she loved cryptic responses. These people were going to be a lot of fun. "Do we have a choice?"

Hilda shot her a side glance. "Isn't that where we *want* to go?"

Behind them, Damian dropped into the jump seat,

rubbing his hands together. "We really do," he said. "Gun it."

"You're not the captain," Hilda said. If she looked suspiciously at Ivy, she regarded Damian with outright hostility. She'd pushed to restrain him as soon as they returned to the ship, but Sloane didn't see the point; he wanted to go to the Interplanetary Dwellers, had accompanied them of his own free volition, and she couldn't think of a con he might be running. At least, not on her. She didn't see the point in going to all the trouble of setting up a brig for him.

"He's right," Sloane said. "Gun it."

Hilda rolled her eyes, but she pushed the ship forward. Sloane had a feeling the Interplanetary Dwellers would suck them into that Atom station thing no matter what, but it didn't hurt to cooperate.

Sloane released the buckle from her hips. "Guess I'm up. You too, Damian."

Damian winked. "Roger, Captain. Been looking forward to this."

"Not normal," Hilda muttered. Sloane wanted to ask what about her life had *ever* been normal, even before Vin's disappearance, but she managed to restrain herself. Barely.

Ivy was waiting by the gangplank in the cargo bay when Sloane headed down, ready to disembark. Brighton was there, too, somehow always aware of exactly when a mission was set to begin. Sloane was beginning to suspect he might be piping their communications down to engineering.

She'd need to check on that.

To Sloane's surprise, Alex was also waiting by the doors, still wearing her lab coat. "What?" she said, when Sloane gave her a questioning look. "Someone finally gave me some astrophysics work to do. I'm going to do it."

Sloane wasn't sure how much astrophysics help the

Interplanetary Dwellers needed, but she wasn't about to argue. It was just good to see Alex doing something. And not complaining about it.

Damian was the last to arrive, his long coat slung over one arm. He had a half-smile pasted on his lips, but his eyes were glittering. The man had a purpose here. There was no denying that.

Not Sloane's problem. Once she'd dropped him off and gotten the location of Vin's data key from Ivy, he could steal whatever he wanted.

The gangplank opened, and Sloane glanced at Brighton. "Did you do that?"

Brighton shook his head.

The bridge that jutted out in front of them looked like a strip of titanium. And that was it. A thin metal bridge that just...reached out into the black. An open catwalk through the void. It *had* to be surrounded by some kind of invisible tube, but Sloane couldn't see any walls, or even a reflection. Someone must have just scrubbed the windows.

Ivy moved confidently onto the bridge, taking several steps with no apparent ill effects, and Sloane exchanged a glance with Brighton. He shrugged, then moved as if to cross next—and would have, had Alex not practically shoved him out of the way so she could barrel onto the walkway.

"It's a stasis gate." Alex spoke reverently, her tone hushed, as if she were stepping into a museum. "These are theoretical. No, *hypothetical*. A step past wishful thinking."

Clearly not, but Sloane kept that thought to herself.

"Look at the source," Brighton said, his tone matching Alex's for enthusiasm, his trepidation replaced with open awe. "It's a slide adherent. It's not even attached to *Money-maker*'s hull."

"It's really not!" BRO said. It sounded equally enthralled, though it might just have been mimicking Brighton. Tough to tell with those two.

Whatever it was, a sliding adherent did not sound very permanent, or safe. But there was no point in voicing that opinion. Ivy had already finished her tightrope-walk across the vacuum, stepping out of the murder tube—Sloane would refuse to call it anything else, and the evidence could go to hell—and into a green-walled cube.

Apparently fully satisfied as to the safety of this thing, Alex and Brighton followed, with Damian close behind, sauntering across the bridge like he'd built it himself.

When Sloane convinced herself to step out of *Money-maker*'s hull, her feet landed on solid metal. So far, so good, even though every cell in her body was freaking out at the sensation of walking unprotected through the vacuum. She should be floating, and the air should be shooting out of her lungs to dissipate into the abyss; her saliva should be boiling on her tongue, and her body knew it.

But nothing happened. The air was breathable, and her blood didn't freeze-slash-boil inside her veins.

Sloane—who very obviously liked the murder bridge least of all of them, by the way—was the last one to enter the cube. As soon as she did, the walkway retracted back to the station, and the cube's wall solidified into a milky green wall. Seemingly out of nowhere.

Who *were* these people, and what other kind of tech did they have? *Was* this tech? Or was it magic? Sometimes Sloane didn't think there was much of a difference.

"This is where they scan for weapons and search the contents of your fliptabs and eye screens," Ivy said, while the walls pulsed with friendly green light.

"Neat!" BRO said. Still with them. Good to know.

Sloane felt the need to clutch her fliptab close to her body. Not that it would help her. "They can't hack my thoughts, can they?"

"Not that I know of." Ivy's tone was far too serious for Sloane's comfort. "But you might as well know now. There are no secrets on the Atom."

Damian nudged Sloane's elbow. "Don't worry. There's a few."

Sloane shoved him away. "And if you weren't here, I'd have no idea my privacy had just been violated."

Ivy straightened the hem of her blouse. "We don't get many visitors."

With the scan complete, the interior door of the Atom parted to admit them into the halls.

As soon as they were all inside, the corridor....shifted. It was the only word Sloane had for it; one moment, they were standing with *Moneymaker* at their back, its shape plain beyond the green-tinted wall, and the next they were rising, their feet mercifully remaining on the rotating ground as the passage clipped back into place. Though that did not stop Sloane's stomach from rotating uncomfortably along with the sudden change in direction.

When the movement stopped and Sloane dared to twist for a glance out the window, the view had changed. *Moneymaker* was gone.

"You couldn't have briefed us on any of this, Ivy?" Sloane asked, but her client just shrugged, and Sloane supposed that even Ivy couldn't have expected the ship to get yanked out of the Current unexpectedly like that.

"We've been in weirder places," Alex said, though her cheeks looked a bit green.

"It *is* in the name," Damian said. "The Atom. Get it?"

Right. Sloane supposed that from the outside, the

rotating spheres would transform the disk into something like an atom.

Brighton was studying every corner of the room, scanning slowly, but not for danger; he looked like he wanted to dive into the guts of this place to understand how it worked.

"Do you really expect me to believe that the Interplanetary Dwellers don't expand on this technology?" Sloane asked Ivy as they started down the newly attached hallways. "That they don't develop it themselves?"

"We really don't," Ivy said.

Sloane shook her head, trying to understand. "But how can the Interplanetary Dwellers be caretakers of technology that's ten times more advanced than anything in the rest of the galaxy?"

"A hundred times more advanced," Alex murmured. Green tint or no, she looked as fascinated as Brighton by their surroundings.

Fans. You couldn't bring them anywhere.

"I don't know," Ivy said. "It's just what we do."

"Or," Damian said, cleaning close over her shoulder as he walked, his voice low, "my stepsister is as brainwashed as every other poor IPD sod who grew up in this place. They develop the tech. Count on it."

"You don't know that," Ivy shot back over her shoulder. "And don't call us—them—the IPD. They hate that."

Damian's smile slipped, but he plastered it back on so quickly that Sloane might have imagined it. "What I do know about the tech is that they don't pull it out of their—"

"Welcome," a voice said, with such a well-timed interruption that Sloane was certain that whoever owned it had been eavesdropping. No secrets on the Atom, indeed.

A pair of pearlescent doors parted before them, and Sloane found herself stepping into an auditorium. She wasn't sure how to feel about the fact that she'd just walked straight onto center stage.

Rows of white-robed people looked down at them from an audience filled with pinkish seats. They sat unnervingly still, backs straight, and Sloane had no way of knowing which one of them had spoken until she spoke again.

"We posted no bounty for Damian Sol, but we're grateful for his return nonetheless." The speaker wore the same white robe as the others, only hers had rings of red fabric marking the cuffs of her sleeves. Did that make her the leader? Did they *have* a leader? She had light brown skin and a sharp chin, her face coming as close to an actual heart shape as Sloane had ever seen.

Damian gave a half bow. "It's Damian Riddle now, thanks."

The woman stared him down, as if she were used to being able to shoot lasers from her eyes and found the ability momentarily, and annoyingly, deactivated.

"He'd not a gift, Amayra," Ivy said. "We're offering him at a price."

Amayra closed her eyes so slowly that it took Sloane a moment to realize she was blinking. "Name your fee, disgraced one."

Subtle.

"The inlays," Ivy said, without hesitating. "I get to keep them."

Amayra gave a shake of her head that looked like a flinch, her hair flowing gently around her face as she moved. "Impossible."

But Ivy had planted her feet squarely on the pearly-pink floor and was now sharing her tight expression with the entire room, scanning the auditorium as she spoke. "The inlays, or we're gone."

Sloane wanted to point out that the Interplanetary Dwellers had all the power here, and that they clearly knew it. She doubted that they'd be willing to just call it a day and let *Moneymaker* leave. Not with Damian, and not with Ivy's tattoos intact.

They'd posted a bounty on Ivy. They wanted to clean up this mess and be done with it.

Sloane cleared her throat. She was hardly a diplomat, she should at least offer Ivy an assist. "Ivy came to me about Damian," she said. "She wanted to help you."

"Yes, we know," Amayra said. Her tone was unnervingly even, the large room adding the ghost of an echo to her words.

"What *don't* you know?"

"Why you agreed to help her."

Damian gasped softly. "*Such* a good question. Now I want to know, too."

Sloane ignored him. "My uncle disappeared," she said. "Before he did, he stole a data key from the Fleet. It might be related and it might...help me find him. Ivy knows where it is, and she agreed to tell me."

"Fascinating," Damian said. Sloane wondered how he'd feel about getting punched in the lip right about now.

The woman twisted to the side, matching Ivy for grace, and exchanged a glance with the man who was seated to her right. Sloane could see other such looks passing among the audience. Passing direct messages via eye screens, she had no doubt.

"My uncle," Sloane said. "Vincent Tarnish."

Amayra turned back to face her. "We know where the key is. But Ivy does not."

To her credit, Ivy cringed.

"Fascinating," Damian repeated.

Sloane sighed. Maybe bounty hunting really wasn't for her. If she could take on a single job without getting double crossed, she'd be so surprised she might keel over in shock before she could collect her payment. "All right," she said, "can *you* tell me where it is? I did bring Damian."

"She did," Damian agreed.

More long glances. More silent eye-screen messages.

"We will need to discuss this," the spokeswoman said finally. "You may go and rest. We've prepared a lounge for your use."

Of course they had. They'd probably known she was coming since before she'd even taken this job. Who the hell *were* these people?

CHAPTER 14

THE INTERPLANETARY DWELLERS seemed determined
to sell the idea that Sloane and her friends were guests, not
prisoners. The lounge they'd provided was a large, circular
chamber, the walls lined with a ring of plush couches. Fruit
and baked goods had been piled onto trays on a round table
in the center of the room, along with a tea service, and
they'd been directed to a bell that could summon assistance
if they needed it.

Only Damian had been fitted with an ankle bracelet
alarm, though judging by the way he was stretched out on
one of the couches, hands propped behind his head, he had
no intention of setting it off.

Then again, maybe the rest of them really weren't prisoners at all. The Interplanetary Dweller council people, or
whatever they called themselves, knew perfectly well that
Sloane wouldn't try to leave until they'd reached a decision
about the data key. Why it was such a contentious decision,
she didn't know, but that only made her more anxious to get
ahold of it.

Brighton and Alex were sitting together by the doors,

examining the room and discussing each detail with deep interest. They were not likely candidates for attempted escape. And the council had kept Ivy with them for questioning, so she was out of the equation.

When Sloane had a chance, she was going to get answers out of the woman. Ivy had promised to pay her for this job with information about Vin's lost key. She'd hinted that there was more to the key than Sloane had considered, and that it could help her solve the mystery of his disappearance.

Ivy had conned her. Completely and fully.

"Your pacing is disturbing my attempt at pretending to sleep," Damian said without opening his eyes. "If you must do it, get me a cookie on your way past the table."

Sloane picked up a cookie and lobbed it at his face. He caught it anyway. "Ugh," he said. "Raisins."

Sloane collapsed onto the couch behind his head, keeping enough distance to save her from errant crumbs. "Are Interplanetary Dwellers all lying bastards?" she asked.

"They're duplicitous by nature," Damian said around a mouthful of cookie. "Why? Known many?"

"Didn't *you* grow up here?"

"Yes, but I've unpacked my trauma enough to speak of them in the third person. I know, my ability to heal is extraordinary. I deny all interview requests, however."

Sloane tapped her fingertips on her knee, an uncomfortable orb of heat expanding in her chest. It felt like pain, like it might explode. "You grew up here," she repeated, without quite meaning to. "Did you know Oliver Crest?"

Damian went still, his expression touched with caution for the first time. "Why? Are you working with him?"

Sloane let out a breath. "He's dead."

Damian tipped his head back so that he was looking at

her upside down, his hair flopping around his face. "You don't sound sorry."

I'm not, Sloane wanted to say, but the words dried on her tongue. "I don't know what I am."

When Oliver had applied to work as her security officer, with limited pay and a dangerous objective, she'd been thrilled. He'd been experienced, and—as she later learned—knowledgeable about the Parse Galaxy's underworld. It'd seemed like a good thing.

Then they'd discovered that he'd deserted from the Fleet and stolen something of theirs in the process. Learned it, in fact, when a Fleet ship came after them and tried to blow them up. Or, knowing what she knew now, tried to disable *Moneymaker* so they could snatch Oliver back, along with their stolen property. But it had seemed like certain death at the time, and Oliver hadn't said anything to correct that assumption.

Sloane should have done something about that particular red flag. The dishonesty was one thing, but she hadn't much cared about his betrayal of the Fleet. She'd felt they deserved it, even. Especially given Vin's earlier suspicions about them. Now... Well, now she wasn't so sure.

In any case, he should have told her. Yes, he'd been embarrassed, or he'd pretended to be at least. He'd explained it away with silver-tongued lies and objection-melting kisses. And she'd let him do it.

But he'd been after Alex's tech all along, and he'd used it to aid the most powerful tyrant in the galaxy.

Then he'd died trying to reverse his actions.

It was all very confusing.

"He betrayed me," she said. "Then he died, and he stuck me with a side quest that almost killed me."

"Do tell."

Sloane slid down further on the seat, letting her legs stretch out in front of her. "Do you have a week? I mean, I guess I should tell you that he tried to rob your father with me. Archimedes tortured him."

And had then chased after them until they'd accidentally escaped into another galaxy. Good times.

"I don't even know who to root for in that story," Damian mused. "I'm genuinely stymied."

Despite the tightness in her throat, Sloane laughed. It came out sounding strangled and wrong, but it relieved some of the tension in her chest. Enough to let her breathe again.

Damian roused himself up to a seating position, the ankle alarm sliding down with a quiet *chink* as he moved. "Look, don't take it personally. Betrayal is—*was*—Oliver's default setting, yeah?"

If he suspected that Oliver had been more to her than a treacherous employee, he didn't say it. A relief, really. She got enough heat on that score from Hilda.

"Is it yours?" Sloane asked. She could think of no other reason why anyone would agree to be a prisoner, would turn himself in like this. She had no idea why Damian would want to be contained. And yet here he was, looking like he'd landed the opportunity of a lifetime. She didn't know what he was after. She wasn't sure he wanted to.

"Who, me?" Damian winked, then propped his hands back behind his head. "I'm a delight."

The doors slid open, and a woman in a white robe entered, her hood raised. Sloane wondered if it meant something, or if she was just cold. It *was* a bit chilly here.

"The stewards have reached a decision," the hooded woman said.

The stewards. How fitting.

They waited in unnerving silence as Sloane filed back onto the stage, Damian a step behind, Brighton and Alex hanging back to drink in every bit of tech they passed. Ivy was waiting for them, fingertips splayed against her hips, an enigmatic smile touching her lips.

Sloane made herself look at Amayra, and the woman met her eyes, her own gaze calm and only a little bit imperious.

"We have agreed that the price is fair," the woman said.

Damian crossed his arms over his chest. "I knew I was worth it."

If the man wanted to convince them he was an actual prisoner, he was going to need to act a bit more contrite. But then, he seemed to know what he was doing. Sloane had enough on her plate without worrying about wayward loner types.

"Ivy may continue to serve as steward to her inlays," the woman said, though the way her eyes raked over Ivy's arms, Sloane had a feeling these people would use any excuse to snatch that permission back.

A pair of hooded Interplanetary Dwellers stepped up to escort Damian away, and he offered them each a small bow before twisting to meet Sloane's gaze. "Default setting," he said. "Don't forget."

For a beat, Sloane's heart went cold. Was he still talking about Oliver? Or was he trying to warn her that Ivy could have cut her out of whatever deal she'd made with the Interplanetary Dwellers?

Ivy couldn't mean to betray her again. She *wouldn't*.

But that was never a given. Not in this galaxy.

And here she thought Fortune was naïve.

The stewards, however, seemed to value honesty. Or the semblance of it, anyway. Otherwise, they'd simply have taken Damian into custody the moment he'd stepped on board. They wouldn't be negotiating at all right now, especially when they seemingly held all the power here.

Sloane turned back to them. She couldn't worry about Damian, not when he was here of his own accord. The way he strode out of the room, throwing a casual wave back over his shoulder, she had a feeling the Interplanetary Dwellers were about to regret his presence here.

"And the data key?" Sloane asked.

The woman nodded, and again Sloane wondered how she knew about it. Why she cared. And why it had been important enough to discuss.

Or maybe it was all a ruse. A performance.

"Your uncle's lost data key is in Cappel System," Amayra said. "It's with Osmond Clay."

CHAPTER 15

SLOANE DIDN'T KNOW why Vin would have given the data key to Osmond Clay. She didn't know that he even had, and she didn't like the coincidental timing of the information—though with everyone busy obsessing over this summit meeting, it might be the best time to sneak in.

She only knew that she didn't have a choice. She had to go to Cappel, and she had to retrieve the key. She was still working on the 'how,' but it'd come to her. It always did.

Hilda, at least, agreed with her. As soon as the Interplanetary Dwellers released them back to the ship—minus Damian, of course—Hilda insisted that *Moneymaker* needed to refuel before they could 'follow Vincent's harebrained trail into the least friendly System outside of the Fringe.' Her words, not Sloane's.

Sloane would have added an expletive.

The place to stock up on fuel and supplies was a barebones waystation at the edge of one of the Outer Systems. From a distance, it looked like a barbell, with fat ends connected by a spindly tube, the whole thing butting up against the Current like a piece of discarded hardware.

There were two reasons Sloane could think of for its existence: resupply for those wanting to deal with honest vendors before diving into Adu System, or resupply for those wanting to deal with honest vendors before diving into the Fringe.

Yes, Cappel was nearby—relatively speaking, and Current-wise—but no one went to Cappel. Ever.

As soon as they docked, Brighton made some noise about needing to tune up various mechanical nuts and bolts. Ivy, who seemed content to stick with *Moneymaker* for the time being, wandered off in the opposite direction, though she didn't appear to have a destination in mind—maybe she wanted to test the Interplanetary Dwellers and their agreement to remove the bounty from her head—while Alex seemed determined to re-stock the pantry after Damian's visit. Apparently the man really *did* like cookies.

Sloane hoped the Interplanetary Dwellers hadn't disposed of him yet. She wasn't nearly as confident as he was in his ability to escape that strange disk of theirs. Though given what she knew from the little time she'd spent with Damian, he could probably charm the walls into parting for him, and convince the vacuum to allow him passage, too.

Brighton and Alex headed off in the same direction, and Sloane watched them leave, hoping the outing wouldn't end with them punching each other over cookie flavors. When choosing between mint chocolate and lemon tang, the answer was obviously *both*.

Sloane hadn't been entrusted with any tasks—nothing as important as cookie purchasing, even—so she decided to stretch her legs out in the station. *Moneymaker* was docked along the middle spine, and Sloane ventured toward the left, following the line of mostly empty bays to a similarly empty rotunda of shops. No wonder this place hovered right outside the Current like a hungry shark waiting for a fish. Seemed pretty starved for customers.

The halls reminded her vaguely of the black-market station she'd visited once with Oliver, though this place was decidedly emptier than that one had been. Most of the stalls and shops here were staffed by androids, and they didn't seem to care whether or not she entered their establishments. The few human vendors she passed didn't even bother to look up from their fliptabs when she walked by.

Maybe they weren't as desperate for business as it seemed. The shopkeepers were probably running feed-based casinos on their fliptabs and making triple what they earned here.

Or they were getting paid to watch drama vids.

Sloane paused in front of a window display full of laser pistols. Hers was still stuck on the stunner function, and while she still didn't relish the idea of murdering anyone, there were times when a good hot bolt of heat might get her out of a tough situation. She was about to leap headlong into the most insular System inside of the Fringe. Might be time to upgrade her firepower.

She ventured into the shop, where the android shopkeeper stood eerily still behind the counter as it welcomed her in a voice that sounded like chimes. The place smelled like rubber and grease, an undercurrent of char suggesting that someone had been testing weapons in here recently. Or stealing them, perhaps.

Sloane was starting to peer over the display, wondering if she had the funds to actually purchase anything—and whether the android was programmed to make fun of her if she asked a stupid question—when a hand came down to rest on the case beside her.

"I recommend the 460 model. Minimal kickback, but enough punch to get your point across."

For absolutely no reason—no reason at all—Fortune's voice set off a riot of fireworks in her chest. She hadn't even looked up from the case, and she already felt her traitorous lips trying to form a smile. Like the Commander of the Galactic Fleet was a *friend*.

The last time she'd seen him, he'd called her capable. Exasperatingly capable, sure, but the exasperating part was almost a point of pride at this point. A calling card.

No one called her capable. Exactly no one.

And in the week or so that had passed since they'd parted...well, she hadn't expected to speak with him at all, let alone twice. She hadn't expected him to contact her simply because he'd seen some of her antics on the feeds.

But he had. And now there were little bombs pinging off the inside of her ribcage.

He'd startled her, she told herself. That was all. She took a moment to finish perusing the guns, pretending to consider the 460 before straightening to look him in the eye.

The first thought that came into her mind was that he looked tired. She studied him, trying to figure out where the impression came from when he was standing there looking as imposing as ever, his back straight, his midnight blue Fleet uniform pristine. It was something in his complexion, maybe. A dullness in his eyes. Like he'd seen something he wanted to forget, and it was haunting him.

Sloane rested a hand on the case, imitating his posture. She was going for casual, though she had a feeling she just looked ridiculous. "Fortune," she said. "What a coincidence. Not following me, are you?"

"Oh, I absolutely am." He smiled, but it did little to ease

the weary lines around his eyes. "We caught your ship's transponder signal."

"And you what, decided to drop in for a chat? Missed me that much, did you?"

Fortune dropped his gaze to the weapons in the case, examining them with what was no doubt an expert eye. "Your zapper's a bit rundown."

Sloane propped a fist to her hip, offended on behalf of Vin's rickety old weapon. "Zapper?

"That's what we call the older hand models. The direct upgrade would be a laser fusion shooter." He touched a fingertip to the left side of the case, indicating a sleek black weapon with a squared-off barrel.

Sloane pointed to the display case on the wall behind the android's diamond-shaped head. "But I like that one."

Fortune squinted at it, though he couldn't be having any trouble making it out. The thing was as long as her arm. "That's an astral fusion rifle."

"Yeah. Looks powerful." And heavy. But she could handle heavy.

"We call it the Regret," he said. "Trust me, you don't want to be walking around with that thing. Not unless you're sure your enemy doesn't plan to show any mercy."

"Could be useful."

"Could be deadly."

Sloane dropped her fist from her hip and tapped the case, signaling to the android. "I'll take a laser fusion shooter."

"Good call," Fortune said.

She'd have liked to ask what kinds of extras the shop might have in the back—a trick she'd learned from Oliver—but she didn't want to do that with Fortune watching. He might not argue, but then again, he might decide to shut the place down. It was tough to predict, with him.

She'd have to swing back later for another look.

The android scanned her ident and payment information. "Your background is clear," it said. "You are free to make your purchase."

Fortune stared the android down like it was a misbehaving student. "I assume that was for my benefit," he said.

"We adhere to Cadence System weapon-purchasing guidelines, Commander." The android actually managed to sound affronted, which was an accomplishment given that its voice was more like grinding gears than anything biological. "We do not sell weapons to criminals."

Fortune hitched a thumb in Sloane's direction. "And her background is clear? Really?"

Sloane wondered how the Commander of the Galactic Fleet would react if she punched him in the face.

Also, she wondered if her background really *was* clear, or if the android was lying. Could androids lie? Would this one lie, just to make a sale? It seemed unlikely.

The android placed the fusion shooter into Sloane's palm. It was lightweight, at least compared to Vin's old stunner-stuck zapper—what a humiliating nickname—and it didn't have so much as a single spot of rust.

"Shiny," she said. "I'm going to name her Louise."

Fortune's eyebrows twitched. "All right," he said. "So, what are you doing out here?"

There really were only two reasons a person might come here, and they both involved some of the sketchiest parts of the galaxy. Of course, Fortune might well be headed out to Cappel for that summit thing, but he had no reason to suspect that she would be.

"Are you going to preemptively arrest me?" she asked. "Because I'm not going to do anything illegal."

Probably, anyway.

"I don't preemptively arrest people, Ms. Tarnish."

He waited, his question still hanging between them. Did she want to tell him? Expose her plan? She couldn't think of a reason why she shouldn't, unless he really was involved in some galactic takeover conspiracy.

But that seemed less and less likely by the day. It was easier to believe, in fact, that he was being duped by some genius underling in the Fleet and that the whole empire bid that Vin had believed so wholeheartedly in would turn out to be the brainchild of a disgruntled assistant to the assistant of Fleet supply chains, or something like that.

Fortune already knew she was looking for Uncle Vin. She couldn't see how he could possibly stop her.

Or maybe she wanted to trust him, just a little too much.

"I'm going to Cappel," she said. "They have something that's mine, and I want it back. Why? Did you finally decide to go to this important summit party?"

Fortune didn't look surprised. He brushed his thumb across the glass case while the android watched from behind the counter. It would remain completely still until they asked for more help. Or until they tried to steal something, at which point she was fairly certain it would obliterate them.

If Fortune tried to steal something, Sloane thought she might die of shock.

"It occurs to me that our purposes might be aligned once again," he said finally. "Would you like to add some stealth tech to your ship?"

CHAPTER 16

BY SOME SILENT or routine agreement, *Moneymaker*'s crew were all packed together in the half-circle booth in the galley, every one of them eyeing Gareth with mistrust. All except Sloane, anyway. Not that he was unused to suspicion, particularly from those who dipped their toes into underworld dealings, but his enemies usually stared him down from a more intimidating vantage.

Under less sobering circumstances, the crew's uniform concern would have been almost comical.

Brighton Walsh was much too big for the booth, particularly since he'd taken the deepest seat, which meant he was hemmed in on all sides by the others. The table pressed into his gut, which had to be uncomfortable, and he was watching Gareth with wary eyes, like he expected to be hauled away to a Fleet ship at any moment. To his left, a woman with black skin and the pearly inlays of an Interplanetary Dweller sat with a similar expression on her face, though Gareth didn't know who she was or why his presence might worry her.

He did know that he'd never seen activated inlays like

that outside of the Interplanetary Dwellers' home station, which he'd visited only twice. He found himself very much wanting to know the rest of her story.

Moneymaker's redheaded scientist was tucked into the booth beside the Interplanetary Dweller, eyes narrowed, while the pilot with the long gray braid had her arms crossed over her chest. Her gaze danced back and forth between Gareth and the Interplanetary Dweller, as though she couldn't quite decide which one of them might betray the crew first.

Interesting dynamics.

As for Sloane, she'd pulled herself up on the counter across from the booth—a wise choice, unless she wanted to sit on someone's lap—with her back to the various cooking appliances. She sat with her long legs crossed in front of her, and she leaned back into her palms to brace herself on the counter. It looked at once casual and uncomfortable. She, at least, wasn't glaring at him.

"All right," she said, "let's hear this plan of yours."

Doing his best to ignore the collective suspicion of the crew, Gareth risked stepping closer to the booth so he could set his fliptab on the table, then projected a miniature model of the plan. It was a far cry from *Sabre*'s strategy room, but it would do.

"We'll get *Moneymaker* into Cappel by applying stealth technology to the hull," he began.

The pilot, Hilda, let out a huff of breath. "Short memory, Commander. The Federation saw right through your stealth tech when we were in Pike, didn't they?"

Oh, he remembered. "We don't know that for sure," Gareth said. "They might have been following us, or making a guess. And we're going to Cappel, not Pike. If the

Federation *can* see through our tech, there's no reason to assume they'd share that knowledge."

"But you're going to the trouble to cause a diversion," Brighton said, his voice a low grumble in the back of his throat.

Gareth nodded, twitching his fingers to call the Fleet ships into the model. "We'll send a pair of visible frigates to keep the Cappel officials busy, on the off chance that they *can* see through your stealth tech. Get them looking in the wrong direction."

Hilda grunted. "It's a hell of a good con technique for someone who claims to be above reproach."

Gareth tucked his hands into the small of his back. He didn't expect these people to submit to his command, but he'd be lying to himself if he didn't admit to feeling a bit ungrounded here. Out of his element. "I never claim to be above reproach," he said. "And I've seen a good share of cons, albeit from the other side."

Sloane actually smiled at that. Hilda muttered something under her breath, unconvinced.

"Once we get close, Fortune and I will rocket down to the surface," Sloane said. "Brighton and Ivy will stay here and use their technological wiles to find us a way in through the mines. Alex, can you get Ivy's inlays fixed in time?"

Alex tapped her fingertips on the table. "I think so."

Gareth felt like the conversation was racing three steps ahead of his comprehension. He raised an eyebrow. "What happened to her inlays?"

"They glitched out on Scope," Sloane said. "That vid you saw? Striker waved some magic wand and prevented Ivy from taking over his modded guys. It was really annoying."

Ivy nodded in agreement. Hilda was pressing her

fingertips to her forehead, as if she'd rather have kept this knowledge between them.

Gareth held up a hand. "Are you saying that Ivy's inlays can control bio-implants?"

"Any nearby technology, really," Ivy said.

Gareth knew he was staring—gawking, if he was being honest with himself—but he couldn't help it. No wonder he'd never seen Interplanetary Dweller inlays lit up like that. They must only be activated when they were on the Atom.

He could see why.

Sloane gasped, eyes wide. "Fortune," she said. "Did we know something you didn't?"

Gareth laced his fingers together behind his back. "I thought the Interplanetary Dwellers didn't use their technology outside of the Atom."

It was a decision his father had tried to negotiate away, in favor of distributing their advancements across the galaxy. Gareth had dropped that mission when he'd taken command. The Interplanetary Dwellers didn't hurt anyone with their technology, and as long as they kept it that way, he'd seen no reason to press them.

He had his own advanced tech labs, after all, and he hadn't seen any evidence that distributing that kind of technology indiscriminately across the galaxy—especially when one didn't know exactly what it entailed—would improve anything. It would only cause more headaches.

Besides, the Interplanetary Dwellers had been firm; they saw themselves as caretakers, and that was that.

Ivy shrugged a delicate shoulder, leaning back in the booth. "I'm special."

Gareth looked at Sloane. "Does anyone on this ship know what modesty looks like?"

"Yeah." She grinned. "You're lucky we let you hang out with us at all, Fortune."

What would Lager say about the plan, and Gareth's presence here? He might object, but then again...then again, Gareth could see him fitting in here, falling in with the crew like they were old friends. He found himself wishing he could see that.

Well, he would. They'd go to Cappel, they'd find Lager, and he'd get to see what was so intriguing about this little freighter and its crew.

Though Lager *had* sent him that video. Perhaps he already knew.

Hilda leaned her forearms on the table, her attention still locked on the model. "Let me make sure I understand. Brighton and Ivy are going to guide Sloane and the Commander into the mines so they can infiltrate a party that he's invited to anyway and could easily access through the front door."

Gareth lifted a finger. "Wasn't actually invited."

"So not without getting murdered," Sloane said.

At least someone understood.

"Details," Hilda muttered.

Sloane pointed at the model. "Then we find our way up, I retrieve Vin's data key, and Fortune—" Sloane waved her fingers in his direction. "—does whatever it is he's going there to do."

"We should find that out," Ivy said. "Maybe."

A fair question. "My ships have been disappearing, and we tracked one of them to the outskirts of Cappel," Gareth said. "I need to investigate that."

"Right," Sloane said. "Missing battleships, bad. They have big guns."

"And hundreds of soldiers on board," Gareth added.

Sloane nodded. "So Fortune's going to ask nicely for them to please stop stealing his toys," Sloane said. "And then we'll escape."

"That's your extraction plan?" Hilda asked. "'And then we'll escape?'"

"Fortune's got rockets, and you're an ace pilot. We'll figure it out." Sloane winked, and Gareth thought Hilda might be considering punching her captain in the nose.

Hilda opened her mouth to speak—or argue—but Sloane slid off the counter and brushed her hands together. "No time for a discussion," she said. "This is the plan. Hilda, I need you on the pilot's deck. Alex and Ivy, get to work on those tattoos. Inlays. Whatever they are. Brighton might be able to help—"

"He definitely can*not* help," Alex interrupted.

"—so he should join you in the lab, too," Sloane finished, ignoring Alex's objections. "We only have a few hours, guys. This is our chance to get Vin's data key, and maybe to find out where the hell he disappeared to, so go."

They went. Without so much as an eye roll, too. Gareth thought, not for the first time, that this woman could command the Fleet itself, if she wanted to.

Only Hilda paused on her way to the pilot's deck, and it wasn't to question Sloane's instructions. She planted herself in front of Gareth, and even though her head barely reached his shoulder, she managed to seem like she was looming over him. "How much are you paying us for this job?" she asked.

He couldn't blame her for trying, really. "I outfitted your ship in stealth technology," he replied.

Hilda raised a finger like she meant to poke him in the chest. "I want assurances that you are aboveboard."

"Hilda, this man couldn't lie to save a baby kitten," Sloane said wearily. "Let it go."

Hilda, he suspected, had no intention of letting it go. She didn't look away; she just stared him down, finger hovering an inch from his chest, until he said, "Are you this suspicious of everyone?"

She dropped her hand. "Yes."

Somehow, she made it sound like a threat.

And then she was gone, threading her way through the storage room that ran between the galley and the flight deck.

Sloane was standing in the middle of the kitchen, watching her people obey her orders with a bemused look on her face. Like she couldn't quite believe they'd actually done what she asked.

"If I recall," Gareth said, "it's actually *my* data key you're going after."

Sloane snorted and turned her back on him, firing up the kitchen gadget she claimed had come from another galaxy. "Finders keepers."

She hadn't found it so much as she'd swiped it right out of Captain West's outstretched hand—kind of—but all right. "Oh, good," he said. "I'll let Osmond Clay know you said that. And just so you know, I'm perfectly capable of fibbing when baby kittens are at stake."

"You're not helping yourself, Fortune. Coffee?"

He found himself taking a step closer and stopped, resting a hand on the counter instead. "Will you be offended if I admit I don't like it?"

She'd shared it with him last time, and he'd found the taste to be overwhelming. Intriguing, though, and intense. The few sips he'd taken had left him feeling jittery.

Not unlike the feeling of spending time with Sloane Tarnish, come to think of it.

"Um, no," she said. "You'll just save me from fighting you for it when I run out."

He watched her flip the switches on her machine, closing her eyes and inhaling deeply as the dark liquid splashed into her mug. "Your Lieutenant friend," she said, "he let you come here all by yourself?"

Gareth swallowed hard. He couldn't let himself get distracted here. "He's on one of the missing ships."

Sloane opened her eyes and twisted to look at him, sympathy clear and shining in her dark eyes. "I'm sorry."

Gareth nodded. He'd been trying not to spend too much time thinking about what Clay—it *had* to be Clay— had done with Gareth's soldiers. The ships could be replaced, but his people could not. And Lager's disappearance was a knife to his gut, a wound that would not close until he'd saved his friend.

He didn't want to dwell on it. He needed to act, not wallow. Casting around for a change of subject, Gareth found himself wondering why Damian Riddle wasn't on *Moneymaker*. Or at least, he didn't appear to be. Sloane had met him on Scope, maybe even followed him into his strange little underworld. Had they formed a partnership? Or was he down in one of her haphazardly assembled brig crates?

In a way, Gareth didn't want to know how well they'd gotten along. And yet, in a way, he had to.

Curiosity won out. "So, Damian," he said. "Did he charm you into dropping your bounty hunt?"

Sloane shook her head and plucked her mug out from under the machine, taking a long draw before answering. "That man is a mystery wrapped in a..." She circled her wrist, as if searching for the right word. "Clown suit, I think."

Gareth couldn't help it. He laughed. After the last few days, poking through wrecked ships, facing the HTR-79 massacre, and caring for the fierce band of orphans left behind, he wouldn't have thought he still could. But it loosened something in his chest, something that had lodged there and stuck.

The galaxy could be a horrific place, the depths of its tragedies enough to sear the goodness right out of you, if you let it. But if there could still be compassion, and if there could still be laughter, then Gareth would keep on fighting until he filled every corner of it with light. In the end, that was the only mission that mattered.

Sloane looked like she wanted to say more. Before she could, her AI's voice joined in the conversation. "Hilda says to let you know we're about to exit the Current!" it said. "I've never been to Cappel System before! Isn't that exciting?!"

Sloane sighed, took another sip of coffee. "Thanks, BRO," she said. "Let's go see if Vin left any breadcrumbs for us to follow."

CHAPTER 17

SOMETIMES SLOANE WISHED the Currents weren't quite so fast. She did want to get on with the job, steal back Vin's data key and get out of here. Of course she did. Still, she couldn't help wishing there was just a bit more time to prepare.

But they'd stopped to resupply right on the border of the Cadence-Adu bands, and the trip to Cappel was a quick one. Just a hop, really. Now, as they made their tentative way out of the exit—Sloane pictured the ship tiptoeing into Cappel's territory, a thief in the night—Fortune claimed his frigates were already making friends in Cappel System. Hilda's scanners confirmed that *Sabre* and *Cutlass* were hulking closer to the planet by the minute, clearing the way for *Moneymaker* to make its move.

It was hard for Sloane to believe that they'd truly be able to just waltz into one of the most notoriously secretive systems in the galaxy, but so far no one had attempted to stop them. They were maintaining radio silence, using direct comms only, and Fortune kept casting broodingly anxious looks out the window as if he had the power to hear the conversations between his officers and the Cappel System gatekeepers, if only he concentrated hard enough.

From here, Cappel Planet just looked like a big rock. No terraforming, no buildings, no atmosphere to speak of. Everyone must live in the mines and the surrounding tunnels.

When people called this place habitable, they really were using the term in the broadest possible sense.

Finally, *Moneymaker* glided in close enough for Hilda to shoo Sloane and Fortune down to cargo to prep for their descent to the surface. For some reason, Fortune was wearing a regular atmo suit rather than the battle-ready armor she'd seen him wear for other fights.

He seemed to think diplomacy would still be an option here. Sloane hoped that wasn't a mistake. He was arranging his things in the middle of the cargo bay, extracting his pack from its hard-sided case and checking his gun. Which, Sloane noted, was a far cry bigger than her new shooter.

He moved with expert efficiency, handling his equipment like it was an extension of his body. It was mesmerizing to watch him work, and she found it was difficult to look away.

"Tell me something," Sloane said. "Why *did* you come here alone? You should at least have a trusty bodyguard to watch your back." If not a dozen. These people had already tried to assassinate him once.

Fortune glanced at the wall again. Unless the man had X-ray vision, she didn't see what good it would do. "They need all the support they can get. And fewer feet on the ground means we'll draw less attention."

That made sense. He knew his strategy, that was true enough. For once, she supposed the situation really *did* call for Fortune's presence. She doubted this Clay guy would speak to a proxy.

She wasn't sure he'd speak to Fortune, either, but she could see that he needed to take the risk.

Fortune held up what he called a guidance pack—a fancy term for describing a squarish backpack full of rockets —and gave it a last once-over before clipping it over his shoulders and securing the straps around his waist.

"Where are my rockets?" she asked.

"You don't get rockets. We have to descend in tandem."

Sloane frowned. "I want my own rockets."

"I only brought one pack."

She held out her hand. "Then I'll control it."

He crossed his arm over his chest. "Have you ever operated maneuvering thrusters like this?"

As if that mattered. "How hard could it be?"

"We train Fleet soldiers for three years before we certify them to maneuver into space untethered."

"Then your budget really is overblown, Fortune."

He tapped his fingertips on his elbows. "Tell me this, Ms. Tarnish. Have you ever done a true spacewalk?"

Sloane licked her lips, wondering if she could avoid an honest answer and settling on evasive instead. "Maybe," she said.

He held her gaze, only raising his eyebrows a fraction of a fraction of a tick. Sloane sighed. She refused to admit that no, she'd never done a spacewalk. She *supposed* that rocketing through the vacuum without a tether would require a skilled hand.

"Okay, fine," she said. "You run the rockets. But if there's anything to shoot down there, I get first dibs."

He looked back at her, solemn, but there was a spark of amusement in his eyes. "It's only fair."

They stepped into the airlock together, and he started clipping her suit directly to his, binding them hip to hip. He might be used to working with his soldiers in this position, but it was completely new to her. Even with layers of atmosphere suits between them, it felt intimately close.

His head was bent in concentration, and she found herself captivated by the flecks of gray in his dark hair, the tan patch of skin on the back of his neck. He smelled like leather, strangely, and some kind of earthy soap. As close as they were, she found herself wanting to lean closer, to breathe him in. Like he was some guy she'd been chatting up in a bar, rather than the Commander of the entire freaking Galactic Fleet.

It was madness. It was nerves.

"Your hands go on my shoulders," he said when he straightened. All business, because of course he was. It wouldn't occur to him to be anything else. Sloane snapped her head up, doing her best to look like she had not been staring at him.

"Don't drop your arms," he added, "or you could end up in the line of the rocket fire."

"Wouldn't want that."

He secured his helmet over his head, twisting it to attach it to the suit, and she did the same, mercifully clearing her nostrils of his scent, if not her memory. What *was* that?

"We have direct comms," he said, his voice in her helmet now, "but we'll keep the ship channel silent until we reach the entrance to the mines."

Or at least, the spot where Ivy and Brighton guessed the entrance would be, which they'd based on their knowledge of the galaxy and mines in general, and Sloane didn't know what else. She supposed the

Interplanetary Dwellers must hang out in the bands a lot.

Fortune reached for her hands and pulled them up, arranging them on his shoulders. "Ready?"

Sloane's stomach was a riot of hot bubbles, nerves doing their best to climb through her chest. She sealed her helmet. "Ready."

"Don't worry." His lips were moving mere inches from hers, though they were trapped behind a double wall of airtight plastic. "This is the fun part."

She wanted to make a quip about him not recognizing fun if it danced naked in front of him with a name tag on its chest, but the joke caught in her throat.

The airlock cycled.

Sloane jerked off her feet, and it actually took a concerted effort to keep her hands pressed against Fortune's shoulders instead of throwing them up in a desperate move to call a halt to this whole scheme. She was the bounty hunter who rode from the bottom of drop-cabs and jumped from hov-trains with nothing but a bit of rope and a thread of trust to keep her alive. She bullshitted Federation thugs and took on illegal bounties.

She wasn't, by nature, a nervous person.

But there was something about being in the vacuum that just...well, what person in her right mind *wouldn't* be terrified by the vastness of existence? Especially when they were catapulting through it like a bullet shot out of a gun, untethered and free. If Fortune's rockets sputtered, if any of their tech failed, they could easily be lost in the black.

Fortune tapped her on the shoulder, and she started, jerking her head up to look him in the face.

The man was grinning. It was a full-on, ear-to-ear, laugh-line-inducing beam of a smile, and it changed his entire face. It hadn't occurred to her that he could *make* a face like that, so full of joy. He looked young, maybe as young as he actually was. He looked handsome as hell, if she was being honest.

Sloane's heart caught on the bottom of her ribcage, where it proceeded to skip dangerously between her stomach and her throat. He had absolutely no right to go around looking like that. None.

Fortune ticked his chin to the left, oblivious to her contemplation of his face, and Sloane turned her head to look where he was pointing.

Cappel's star burned in the distance like a red eye, watching as they made their progress toward the surface of the planet. But when Sloane's gaze moved past it, she gasped.

Out here, the stars hung in the ether like overlarge pinpricks of light. They shone silver and yellow, and though it should be impossible, she could almost imagine that some of them were a touch bigger. They might be planets, the ones that were closer to Cappel's sun.

Even from such a close distance—they couldn't be far at all—*Moneymaker* was invisible, at least to her eyes. She couldn't even see a gap in the stars where it ought to be. Out here, the galaxy spread before her like a beautiful sea.

She'd never seen anything like it.

She'd barely had time to register the vastness of it—if she ever could—before Cappel's surface was looming close, and Fortune was angling them down feet-first, twisting the universe on its head. It was beyond strange to watch half of the blackness recede behind a surface of reddish-brown rock, even stranger to experience the shift as the vacuum remained fixed above them, ever watchful.

When Sloane's feet hit the ground, she realized she was

laughing. She was still holding onto Fortune's shoulders, and when she finally wrenched her gaze from the stars to look him in the eye, his expression matched the bubble in her chest. Pure adrenaline.

For a moment, the joy was easy. Uncomplicated.

This, more than anything, had to be why he joined his soldiers in so many ground operations. He acted so reserved, and so restrained, but he *liked* the action. No; it was more than that. A part of him lived for it. She could see it. And she thought she understood him, just a little better.

Fortune dropped his attention to her waist and began separating their atmo suits. She couldn't think of anything to say, could barely remember what words even were, so she just watched, trying in vain to catch her breath.

Unfortunately, the subsequent trek across Cappel's surface put an immediate damper on her giddy joy. Just as well, given that they were about to infiltrate a gathering of important people who might or might not be trying to take over the galaxy.

She'd only be fifty percent surprised if it turned out her own father was in attendance.

Cappel's surface was an unpleasant place for a stroll, and her body felt unnervingly heavy after the exhilaration of the drop. She was no physicist, but it seemed like the rock enforced more gravity than a planet its size should. Then again, maybe it only felt that way in contrast to the weightless joy of zipping through the black.

"Nice place for a big convention," she said after a few minutes of trudging. "I'm sure the richest people in the galaxy will be so glad Clay brought them all here instead of renting out a suite on Ve Station."

Fortune laughed, but it sounded bitter. Almost harsh, and completely at odds with the smile he'd unleashed out there. "As long as Clay keeps them in data chips, I don't think they care."

Sloane suspected they might care a little. She tried to picture her father showing up to an event in a place like this, but now that she'd seen it, the image didn't track. He was too proper, too fussy. He'd get dust on his shoes and leave in a huff. Was Clay really hosting a bunch of the galaxy's VIPs here?

"I'm sure Clay's put together some kind of a fancy door for his guests to make a grand entrance through," Fortune said. Sloane felt like her lungs were going to collapse under the strain of this walk, but he wasn't even a little out of breath. She supposed he'd trained to work in a lot of different environments. "He'll have made it much more palatable. And far away from the entrance of his mines."

She hoped so, anyway.

"I bet he's providing photo booths," Sloane said. "And snacks. Important people really like snacks."

"Who doesn't like snacks?"

"You're an important person," Sloane said. "So your perspective just proves my point."

"Are you trying to tell me you're opposed to snacks?"

"I prefer caviar."

He laughed again, and this time the sound was pleasant and deep. A much better match for that smile of his. It was criminal, the way he kept that thing locked away.

She'd like to see it again, sometime.

Fortune paused, and it took a moment for Sloane to see why. The rocky surface seemed to undulate before them, making it difficult to tell hills from cliffs or mountains. Strange rock formations jutted out of the ground at intervals, but they'd be no good as landmarks; if Sloane found herself wandering out here on her own without maps or tech, she felt certain she'd find herself walking in circles within the first hour.

But Fortune had seen what her eyes had missed—or, just as likely, his instruments had. Up ahead, a cave loomed out of the reddish-brown cliff, a gaping maw that was just a little too round, a little too perfectly shaped, to be natural.

The entrance to the mine. Ivy really had been able to guess right where it would be.

"Open up the wide comm channels," Fortune said. "We're going in."

CHAPTER 18

THEY'D ONLY TAKEN a few steps into the cave before the rock walls swallowed the last of Cappel's reddish light from the surface. Gareth activated the night-vision filter on his helmet, hoping that Sloane had one, too, and led the way into the dark.

The tunnel descended in a gentle slope, easing its way into the planet—though whether this rock really deserved that title was still in question. Too smooth for any natural formation, the ground felt almost slippery underfoot. The opposite of HTR-79's roughly hacked corridors.

"I'm just saying that there are four frequently used layouts for a mine like this." Brighton's voice piped up into his ear suddenly, and Gareth glanced over at Sloane, wondering if she'd had to yell at her crew to get them to include him in their discussion.

She was walking a few paces behind him, and when he turned to check on her, she winked.

The expression on her face during that drop had been something to see. She'd hidden her anxiety behind a thick layer of bravado, but he'd met enough nervous new recruits to see it for what it was. Sloane seemed to think fear was for other people—never for her—and though her tendency to leap before looking did often work out in her favor, Gareth didn't see anything wrong with a healthy dose of caution. It could keep you alive.

The mind tended to revolt against the idea of leaping from a ship and into the vacuum of space. No matter who you were.

But then he'd pointed out the view, and her anxiety had melted into pure amazement. He couldn't forget the way her lips had parted, her eyes wide enough to reflect the stars. Full-on wonder. The expression was etched in his mind.

"Five!" BRO said, responding to Brighton's comment. "You should include underwater facilities!"

"They're not underwater right now," Brighton said.

"Right! Four, then!"

"You've got caged elevators with the operating base on the surface." Ivy's voice was clear and confident, like she'd done this a hundred times. "So we can rule that out. Unless they're invisible, I don't see any buildings on the surface here. Then there are probe drills, but again, those are surface based."

"How do you know all of this?" That was Hilda, suspicion lacing her tone. Gareth was pretty sure she wasn't even supposed to be talking on this channel, but he doubted anyone would try to kick her off.

"Interplanetary Dwellers have to eat too," Ivy said.

Gareth made a note to look into that. The Interplanetary Dwellers never seemed to take over anyone else's resources, though, and band-based asteroids were controlled on a first-found, first-served basis. Most groups registered those claims, but he supposed it wouldn't be surprising if the Interplanetary Dwellers were quietly operating a few mines in the middle of nowhere.

"We're looking at two likely scenarios here," Ivy continued. "In either case, you'll encounter an airlock soon. One's a regular airlock that'll lead directly into the mines. There'll be security, but we want it to be that one."

"Why do we want it to be that one?" Gareth asked.

"Easier to hack." Brighton sounded like he was chewing something crunchy. Cereal, maybe.

No one asked Brighton how *he* knew so much about mining layouts.

"The other option's tied into a floodgate," Ivy said. "Two systems to penetrate, instead of one."

"And there's no way to tell which it'll be?" Sloane asked.

"Not without more information about the composition of the planet, no."

Gareth's knowledge of mining operations was limited at best, but that tracked with the little he'd learned in school. It was the kind of thing Fleet tutors were expected to cover, at least with a cursory lesson or two.

Nothing said Cappel had to set up their mine with the standard layouts though. The more he learned about Osmond Clay, the more certain he became that the man was playing a different kind of game. That might apply to his mines as well.

"And if Cappel's doing things their own way?" Sloane asked, echoing his thoughts.

Ivy made a humming noise. "Then we improvise."

"Or," BRO said, "we run!"

"Not an option," Gareth said. He had to get into the summit. Clay might've replaced half the FAC with his own people, but the rest of them were still original. They hadn't gone running at the first sign of trouble, like Alisa and the others had. Gareth might be able to reason with them.

Or they might've been in Clay's pocket the whole time.

If nothing else, Gareth could grab the man by the collar and shake him until he revealed the location of those Fleet corvettes.

In the end, it might very well come down to politics.

The ground sloped down, a bit steeper now, and Gareth lost sight of the passage ahead as it tipped around a gentle curve.

"This is boring," Sloane said. "I was hoping there'd at least be bats."

"There's no air," Gareth said.

"Vacuum-adapted bats."

"What would they eat?"

"Starlight."

She said it like a joke, but he heard something else behind the words. A glimpse, perhaps, of the art lover he suspected she really was. That romantic streak. She buried it deep. He had a feeling she'd done that long before she'd set out on this quest to find her uncle though. She'd been studying medicine, after all, not art.

The passage straightened out, widening enough for them to walk side by side as the ceiling soared to sudden and dizzying new heights. Gareth could make out a trio of narrow iron doors just ahead, each surrounded by an arch of concrete.

"That doesn't look like an airlock," Sloane observed.

"It's a floodgate," Ivy said.

"But not an airlock!" BRO added. "I've never seen this design before! Isn't that amazing!"

That AI needed a reboot. Or maybe a sedative.

Sloane shook her head. "So Cappel does its own thing. I'm shocked."

It truly was impressive, though. A feat of engineering. The doors rose high above their heads, so high that he thought the *Moneymaker* could fly through this section of tunnel without a problem. The doors were separated from the lower tunnel by a thick step of concrete that rose as high as his waist.

No wonder Cappel had no security stations in these tunnels. This dam looked like it would stop a cannon.

"I'm in," Ivy said.

A cannon, maybe, but not a hacker.

"They've just separated the floodgates from the airlock," she continued. "Must just be a peculiar layout in there or something."

"How do the tattoos work?" Brighton asked. "You get, what, a hunch? A tickle?"

"They're not tattoos, they're inlays," Ivy corrected. "And they're—"

"Let's have science class later," Sloane interrupted. "Kinda trapped here."

A pause. "Right," Ivy said. "Brighton and I are going to trick the computer into thinking there's a flood. That way, it'll open the gates for you."

Sloane propped a hand on the wall, craning her neck to look up at the arches. "Not to be a buzzkill, but isn't there water on the other side?"

"Nope," Ivy said. "There's a catch chamber. The water flows in from other parts of the mine. We can control that."

Gareth glanced at Sloane, who met his eyes and shrugged. "They're the geniuses," she said. "I just work here."

She really did seem to believe that.

A breath passed, and another, and he was just thinking of asking for a status update—if he could figure out how to do that without getting yelled at—when the middle door gave a cranking shudder and began inching toward the ceiling.

Sloane started up the step, using the arch to haul herself up, while Gareth paused, straining to see what lay in the passage behind her. As far as he could see, it was just inky blackness. A thin stream of water trickled along the edge of the step, just a glint of movement. Nothing else moved.

Sloane straightened and planted her fists on her hips, looking down at him. "Coming, Fortune? Or am I crashing this party on my own?"

Something flinched in the background, just a flicker of movement. He couldn't make out what it was. He regretted the way the helmet dampened his natural senses, its external speakers filtering any noise. Smelling the tunnels, or hearing what was going on in them, wouldn't necessarily give him a clue about what awaited them back there. But on the other hand, it might.

He felt like he was blindfolded. Groping in the dark.

At Sloane's feet, the trickle of water thickened.

"Shit," Ivy said.

Sloane twisted, studying the darkness beyond the doors. "Not a comforting word, Ivy."

"There was a reservoir of runoff," Ivy said. "It released when we triggered the flood alerts."

Sloane looked down at her feet, as if considering the trickle of water. "Runoff doesn't sound too bad."

"Brace yourselves," Ivy said. "It's coming at you."

"Brace ourselves where?" Sloane asked. "The walls are smooth!"

Gareth threw his body over the step, shouting for her to

duck and do the same. Which she did, though she waited until the last possible second. When she dropped, she was facing the wrong way, looking out toward him with her shoulders dangling over the step while Gareth dug his hands into the thin depression that'd sealed the closed doors to the floor. It was poor purchase, but it was something. He shifted toward Sloane, scraping along the step to brace himself against her upper body.

The flood came in a single, gushing wave, strong enough to lift his feet straight off the rocky floor of the tunnel. He held onto the step, wishing to everything that he'd worn his full body armor for this. He'd only left it behind because he'd thought it would send the wrong message when he reached the summit. If Clay wanted to pretend Gareth was out to install himself as supreme leader of the galaxy, then showing up in full-on Fleet armor was probably not the way to convince anyone otherwise.

Now, though, he thought he might have done Clay's job for him by eliminating himself.

Seconds passed in a riot of bubbles, his visor streaming worried lines of meaningless alerts across his screen as he braced his upper body against Sloane's. Either the suit would hold, or it wouldn't.

And then, as suddenly as it had rushed down on them, the water receded, dropping Gareth's body gently back to the tunnel floor.

Sloane let go of his arms and sat back, raising a shaking hand to her helmet as if to drag it through her hair, which was tucked under her helmet. Water was sloughing down her gray-suited arms. One more dunking like that, and her suit would start disintegrating. His might, too.

"See?" she said. "Not so bad. Shall we?"

She certainly was determined. If she did manage to find

her uncle, Gareth hoped the man would appreciate her dedication to the cause. At this point, he himself might have gone running in the opposite direction, had he not had his own people to rescue.

He followed her up onto the step, and they started into the tunnel. He very much hoped they'd find an airlock here, and that Ivy and Brighton could work their magic on it without drowning anyone.

They'd barely taken three steps before water began to pool under their feet, faster this time, like a glut of ink spilled from a bottle.

"Ivy?" Sloane said.

"Brace." Ivy's voice was pure panic in his ear. "You need to brace again."

But it was too late. The walls here were smooth as marble, and there was no time.

Sloane was already moving back toward the step, and the wave hit Gareth first, washing him toward her. He tried to grab her hand as the water picked her up, too. The tips of their gloves smacked together, and then the water caught hold of Sloane, shaking her like an animal with its teeth full of prey. Her head slammed against the wall, and he reached for her, straining against the pull of the water. She was so close. She was much too far.

And the water took its chance. It grabbed hold of her and, with one last teasing whirl in his direction—almost close enough for him to reach, to hope—it swept her away.

CHAPTER 19

THE WATER FELT like a living thing as it pulled at Sloane's feet, a monster determined to suffocate her in its grip. Or a pair of monsters determined to rip her apart in a violent tug-of-war. She tried to keep her breaths steady, tried not to panic—she had a helmet on, she had air—but the water whipped her into the wall and back to the floor, shaking dark spots into her peripheral vision.

Breathe, she thought. *It'll pass soon. Like the last wave.*

But this one didn't. It kept tearing at her, somersaulting her down a passage that felt much too long while the minutes ticked by, every single one threatening to tear her suit apart, to finally crack the helmet hard enough to splinter it.

Or maybe her sense of time was off. Maybe every minute in her mind was really a second passing. Maybe it wasn't that bad.

Sloane tried to swim, tried to find something to hold onto as the water swept her down the passage she'd just walked. Worst case, she'd end up on Cappel's surface. She hoped.

A cold trickle ran down her wrist, and her breaths started coming in short, panicked gasps as her body understood what it meant before her brain did.

The suit was leaking. Because of course it was.

The water bashed her into the wall and she groaned, reaching again for a handhold. Anything.

This time, she caught one.

Or rather, it caught *her*. She couldn't see anything through the foam, through the fog in her helmet, and the sound of the water had infiltrated her suit now, gurgling inelegantly in her ear and rendering the comms completely useless. Water trickled down her neck, pooling in the pockets beneath her armpits.

She had a spare few minutes of air left. If that.

But at least she'd stopped rushing through the tunnel.

She managed to force her neck against the current, to catch a glimpse of what had caught her wrist.

It was Fortune, as some clear-thinking part of her brain had known it would be. He wasted no time in fighting the currents to drag her closer, arranging her hands on his shoulders as he'd done when they'd dropped out of *Moneymaker*.

And then, somehow, they were pushing back against the current, the water folding around them like it meant to fight back. The rush of it was still in her ears, but she could hear Fortune's voice behind it, and strains of the person who answered. Ivy? The world was awash with motion and noise, everything muted. Water lapped against her chin, and she wondered distantly if anyone had ever drowned inside a space-suit helmet before.

And then Fortune was pulling her out of the still-storming river and slamming his hand into a panel to close a set of doors that looked deliciously like airlock doors.

Sloane fumbled for her helmet, ripping it off her head as soon as the lights turned green, indicating—she hoped, anyway—breathable air.

Since Fortune was also removing his helmet, it had to be safe enough. Safer that sucking water into her lungs.

"Did you just use your rockets?" she asked. She was breathing hard, lungs heaving, her hair heavy and wet against the back of her neck.

He leaned back, pressing his palms flat against the wall. Somehow his hair was dry, which just meant that the Fleet provided better atmo suits than the *Moneymaker* had in stock. She'd have to go shopping. "I did," he said.

"That was an absolutely mad idea. It could have fried us both."

A half smile. "Yes, well, I simply thought 'What would Ms. Tarnish do?' and that was the first thing that occurred to me."

"Good. You're learning." Sloane tipped water out of her helmet, then dropped it on the ground. The seals were useless, and she was pretty sure the visor had cracked. They'd need to get out of here via ship. No more rocketing through the vacuum, assuming the guidance pack even worked now.

With the danger of drowning behind her, Sloane took a second to scan their new surroundings. They were standing in a wide airlock chamber, the walls lined with the same heartless rock that she'd spent the last few minutes trying to grab to save her life.

The other door, the one that hopefully led into the mines—though it was anyone's guess, at this point—was made of solid titanium or aluminum, or something similarly strong and opaque. She wasn't an airlock-door expert.

"Hey, Ivy?" Sloane said. "Any chance of opening that second door?"

"Glad you're alive," Ivy said, confirming that Sloane's earbud still functioned. A small blessing, and she'd take it. "We're working on it."

"It's code she's never seen before!" BRO said. "Isn't that interesting?"

"No," Brighton and Ivy said together.

Sloane needed a moment to collect herself, anyway. She ripped open the atmo suit's clasp and stripped the thing off, stepping out of it and tossing it into the corner. Fortune might be dry, but she was drenched. And not exactly outfitted for the mission ahead; she had on leggings and a black T-shirt. No armor, no extra air supplies, just glorified pajamas. Already, goosebumps were popping up on her arms.

It could be worse. She could be in her underwear.

"You might need that," Fortune said.

Sloane crouched beside the discarded suit and yanked the weapons belt out of the slits in the fabric, then refastened it around her waist. "It's useless now."

"Space suits aren't made for water."

"Seems like an oversight."

"There's not much moisture in the vacuum." He was looking at her a little too intently, his hair barely mussed by that helmet. It really wasn't fair. "Are you all right?"

Sloane tightened her belt and drew her new fusion shooter, turning it over in her hand and hoping it would still be functional after getting dunked in mine runoff. Who knew what kinds of toxins were in that stuff? And she'd practically been breathing it. She needed a shower. And a trip to the med bay, just in case.

But first, she needed to find Osmond Clay and rip Vin's

data key from his smirky little grasp. The details of which she had to admit she hadn't quite worked out yet. They would come to her as soon as the opportunity arose. They always did.

Fortune was still looking at her, waiting for an answer. If she didn't give him one soon, he might decide to scrub the mission.

If that was even a possibility at this point.

"Oh, yeah, I love a good swim," she said. "Thanks for. You know. Not letting me drown."

He gave her a tight smile, his eyes still locked on her like he was worried she might faint. Which she'd have denied, had she been even a little bit certain that she *wasn't* going to faint. "You've got the keys to my getaway ship," he said.

She snorted. "Right. In that case, I retract my thanks."

"Almost got it," Ivy said.

Fortune stepped forward and held out his hand. For a second, Sloane thought he meant to touch her, but then he tapped the laser gun she was still holding. "Waterproof," he said. "That thing would shoot at the bottom of the ocean."

She nodded and slipped the weapon back into her belt, trying not to be unnerved by how easily he seemed to read her mind. "Good to know."

Instead of moving away, he raised his eyes to look into hers. She wondered if he realized how intense his gaze was, then decided he wasn't the sort of person who thought about the arresting power of his own eyes. They were gray, in a stormy kind of way. Not brooding, just...uneasy. Attentive.

Damian Riddle would think of something more poetic to describe his own looks. But not Commander Fortune.

Unless he was running a very good con. She'd barely skimmed the surface of Parse's underworld, but it was enough to remind her that there was always that possibility. Could this man really be a part of that world? She couldn't picture it.

He was probably just trying to read her mind, or make sure she wouldn't turn into a liability after that dunking. Or get a read on whether she meant to betray him.

The doors shuddered, then parted, and Sloane turned away from him to face them. She wasn't sure if she was relieved or disappointed.

When they opened, she wished she'd kept her gun at the ready.

The people on the other side were ready for them. And they were armed.

CHAPTER 20

FOR A SECOND, Gareth was sure Clay had anticipated everything. Their farce with the frigates, their stealthy entry in the mines, all of it. Why else would he be staring into a dozen gun barrels of varying sizes, and more broad-shouldered guards than he would have expected to find in the whole station? There had to be a hundred of them, maybe more.

They held their guns like they meant it, too.

Gareth really should have worn his full armor. He still might not have survived, not at this range, but he'd have had a better chance of getting Sloane out.

Instead of shooting him, one of the guards called back over his shoulder. He looked confused as the group shuffled, then parted, making way for someone who must be their leader. Clay himself? Some high-level crony?

And then Lieutenant Martin Lager stepped out of the crowd. He wore a stiff gray miner's uniform, identical to the ones on the people still holding Gareth and Sloane at gunpoint, and thick black boots that reached halfway up his calf.

No wonder they held their guns like they meant it. They were Fleet soldiers.

Gareth's mind scrambled to reconcile their presence down here, their dirty faces. Had Clay put them to work mining down here?

"Stand down," Lager said. "Let's not shoot the Commander."

Gareth didn't know if they'd called Lager forward to confirm his identity, and what it might mean that they'd been uncertain. A question for later; now, he didn't think he'd ever been so happy to see anyone in his life. He clapped his friend hard on the back to the tune of the rest of the soldiers—they were his soldiers, they had to be, even if they hadn't stood down as soon as they'd seen him—clipping guns and weapons back into holsters and belts.

Lager was grinning, ear to ear, though his face looked drawn and tired, his eyes rimmed in red. "Wasn't sure you'd find us, sir," he said.

"I'm going to admit it was mostly an accident that we did. The last message you sent showed an origin point near Cappel, so we sent a pair of frigates to distract the gate-keepers while we snuck in on Ms. Tarnish's freighter."

Lager looked impressed. "Bold."

"I do my best."

He wondered how the frigates were holding up out there, whether any fire had been exchanged. They were meant to avoid a fight, but what if Cappel had some hidden rail guns out on one of their asteroids? It was a strong possibility.

Sloane was frowning. "I have a really bad feeling about this," she said. "It feels like a trap."

Lager gestured to the room at his back, a wide area with arched ceilings and orange-tinted lighting. "He's had us working down here. We're all here, sir. The *Dirk*'s crew, and the *Hunter*'s."

"And the cube-ship I distinctly remember warning you not to take."

Lager nodded, still grinning. "Yes, sir. That's right."

Sloane was hanging back, hands on her hips as she studied the group of soldiers. "Surely there are easier ways to staff his mines than kidnapping Fleet ships."

"He wanted the ships," Gareth said.

"That's our guess," Lager agreed. "We were going to use the summit as an excuse to escape."

Sloane kept scanning the soldiers, most of whom had shifted into parade rest positions. Gareth wondered if they even realized it. "Have you seen Clay down here?" she asked.

"Not personally, no," Lager said.

She was still frowning, a delicate crease deepening between her eyebrows. "Where are the other workers?"

"They keep us separated," Lager said. "Isolated. Some of us think there might have been an accident and that conscripting miners is just a useful side effect of scooping up Fleet ships."

Gareth wasn't sure what Sloane was getting at with this line of questioning, though surely there were far easier ways to staff a mine. Even in Cappel, where lips were tightly clamped. Plenty of workers went from mine to mine and could be easily enticed from one job to another with the right paycheck. Mines ran dry all the time, or deals went sour. There were plenty of resources.

In all likelihood, Clay had just needed a place to stash the Fleet soldiers while he stole their ships.

"But he has you all together down here," Sloane said.

Lager shot a glance back over his shoulder, then shuffled

a step closer. "Look, my theory is that Clay was—is—planning to dispose of us after the summit. Day or two after it ends, there'll be an explosion down here. Tragic. And secret, since Cappel doesn't share a damn thing with anyone."

Sloane nodded slowly, as if that tracked more closely with her idea of the trap. But she was gnawing at the inside of her cheek, like something didn't quite add up.

At this point, Gareth knew better than to question the woman's instincts. Something about the situation was bothering her. He leaned in closer, aware of his soldiers' eyes on him. "What are you thinking?"

She gave her head a little shake. "I can't put my finger on it. Something's off. I think..." She shook her head again. "I think someone knew you wouldn't come barreling in here just to recapture some ships. I think your people are bait."

Lager pressed his thumb to his lip, looking thoughtful, and Gareth couldn't dismiss the idea. But in the end, it didn't matter. They were here, and they had a job to do.

"We still need to get up to the summit," Gareth said. "Clay owes us both an explanation."

"Double confrontation?" Lager said. "Excellent."

Sloane stepped up beside him, and when he turned toward her, she was looking into his eyes with an earnestness he hadn't seen from her before. "You have your people," she said. "Maybe you don't play into his hands. Maybe you get the hell out of here."

A suggestion of restraint from Sloane Tarnish? She must truly be worried.

He had the sudden urge to grab her hand, to pull her closer to him. It wasn't lost on him that she could have died in that flood. The panic of it had barely receded from his chest.

He cleared his throat. "I can't let Clay keep those Fleet ships. He could cause too much damage. And you saw the imposter ships on Olton Moon yourself." Please, let her believe they'd been imposters. "That wasn't us, which means someone's doing a hell of an impersonation."

She stared at him, like she could read the truth in his eyes. He didn't think she quite believed him, and he didn't know how to convince her. "Maybe there's another way," she said.

"We're here now. Are you giving up on your data key?"

She looked away. "No."

"Then we go in. Together."

Ivy's voice piped up into Gareth's earbud, as if she'd been waiting for them to finish the conversation before interrupting. "Hilda says we can extract the soldiers to *Moneymaker*."

"Cargo's going to be so crowded," Sloane murmured. But she didn't sound upset about it. She was glancing around the mine, as if she wanted to drink in every detail of the spot. As if that might help her solve whatever mystery was knocking around in her brain.

Gareth trusted her instincts, but it didn't change anything. They needed to make their way to the summit, and they needed to confront Clay. Preferably in front of an audience.

There wouldn't be another chance.

"I can get them back out through the airlock, if they've got helmets," Ivy said.

Lager tugged on a hood that was attached to the back of his suit. "Inflates. Lots of jobs to do on the surface."

"Great. All of you head back out," Gareth said. "We've got a freighter and a pair of frigates in the wings."

"If they're not too busy arguing with Clay's gatekeepers," Sloane said.

"With respect, sir, I think you could use another set of hands. I'm coming with you." Lager's tone was light, but his jaw was firm, his wide-set stance suggesting he was ready to die on this hill.

"You've been through a lot," Gareth replied carefully. The last thing he wanted was another argument about who should be involved in ground operations and who shouldn't. "Maybe—"

"Fortune," Sloane said, "if you're going to insist on going up there, we need all the help we can get."

Gareth looked back and forth between them, wondering if they'd made some sort of secret pact to fight him on any he decision made to keep them safe.

Lager was a good fighter and a brilliant tactician, not to mention an excellent leader. Gareth would be a fool to bench him when he said he was well enough to help with the mission. "When you're right, you're right," he relented. "Get everyone into the airlock. It's time to finish this."

CHAPTER 21

IT WAS something of a surprise to see Fortune allowing someone to help him, but Sloane didn't think it was the right time to question him on it. Not when he'd agreed to let one of his well-trained soldiers come with them on this little mission.

They were going to need Lager's help, even if she was wrong about this being an elaborate trap. The heavy pit in her stomach said she wasn't, but she could hope it was just nerves.

Lager led them across the open space, where shelves packed with machines and mining tools—at least, she assumed the collection of picks and drills were mining tools —obscured the walls. He stopped by a narrow door that was set with metal studs.

"This is the exit," he said. "There's a pair of guards that watch it, but we think they're short on backup because of the summit."

Fortune withdrew his weapon from the back of his belt, the gun coming loose with a businesslike click. "Is that a data-based guess or a hope-based one?"

Lager readied his weapon, too. "Hope-based, sir. Pure conjecture."

Fortune nodded. "We work with what we've got. On three?"

He spared a glance at Sloane, who was still trying to work out the back-and-forth between the two men. She nodded and freed her own shooter, hoping that Fortune had been making a data-based guess when he'd said it would still work after getting dunked in a flood.

"On three," Lager said.

The men opened fire on the lock, moving in a coordinated rhythm that showed plainly how long they'd been working together. Lager kicked the door open, and then they were storming out, shouting incomprehensibly for whoever was out there to get down or freeze, or whatever military types yelled when they wanted to raid a facility run by a potentially evil conspirator.

Sloane followed, trying to add a saunter to her walk. Maybe she should have left with the other soldiers. She was hardly needed here. Also, she was going to make fun of them for this later.

Especially since there were no guards waiting on the other side of the door. Fortune had dropped his gun to his side, though he still stood with his muscles coiled tight, primed to raise it again at the first sign of movement.

Lager was looking around, glancing at the ceiling as though the guards might've leapt up there to hide from their shouting. "There are always guards," he said. "Always."

They'd emerged onto a kind of landing, with a single set of stone steps that led up, she assumed, out of the mines. There were no guards in sight, and no footsteps running toward them after that incredibly loud entry into the space. The place was bare.

"Maybe they really are shorthanded." Fortune didn't sound like he believed his own words as he nodded to the stairs. "Up we go."

He and Lager took the lead, and Sloane didn't argue. The Commander was practically crackling with energy—she could feel it radiating from him like electricity—and she wondered how often he really got to be the first to barge into dangerous situations. There was something so restrained about him, so...proper wasn't quite the right word. Intellectual, almost. Reserved.

As she made her way up the steps, her legs already burning, she tried to picture someone else in charge of the Fleet. Someone who showed less restraint, or more eagerness to put his battleships to use. Someone who recruited a more vicious brand of officer.

There was a reason his soldiers protected him. A good one. He might like the adrenaline of a good fight, but he didn't run in without good reason. And he didn't misuse his power.

If the Fleet really was masterminding some kind of galactic takeover plan, Gareth Fortune was not involved in it. He wasn't running a con. He wasn't part of some secret Parse underworld. She knew it in the same way she knew Vin's data key would lead her to him. The same way she knew this was a trap.

And, Sloane had to admit, it didn't seem likely that someone else could carry out such a plan with Fortune at the helm. He didn't miss much. Not to mention the fact that the man had gone tearing off across the galaxy because a couple of his ships went missing. Another person might write it off, or leave it for his spies to handle, but he knew what those guns could do, who they might hurt, and he held himself responsible.

Uncle Vin had been wrong about the Fleet. She accepted that now. But whatever he'd learned from that data key, he hadn't passed it on to the Federation—his employers. Why? Were they in bed with Cappel? Was this whole conspiracy really about taking down the Fleet?

As they ascended, the faint smells of sawdust and recent soldering reached Sloane's nose, growing stronger the further they went. Like they were heading into a construction zone. The staircase had no turnoffs, no landings or passages cutting off to the sides. It was just a single, wide, endless set of stairs that seemed like it wanted very much to kill her.

"Have you been climbing this every day?" she asked Lager, annoyed when her words came out in little huffs. This was not an ideal way to head into a fight.

"Every day," Lager confirmed. Unlike Sloane, he did not sound out of the breath in the slightest. Fortune probably made his soldiers do fifty laps a day, and in double-heavy gravity.

It felt like an eternity before the end came into view, in the form of a door that loomed above her head like a gateway to another world. In a story, anyway. She'd been through an *actual* gateway to another world, and it'd been more like a window of eye-searing light that just happened to be sliced through the web of reality.

Again, Fortune and Lager did their little shoot-the-door-then-blast-it-down dance.

This time, the door blasted straight into a person. Sloane heard it thud, the guard staggering back—bad design, though the makers must have been thinking of keeping people *out* of the mines rather than in—and by the time she pushed herself to the top of the stairs, Lager had the guy standing against the wall, hands raised.

He looked young, like someone had stationed the rookie at this door because he couldn't be trusted with anything else.

"Where is everyone?" Sloane asked.

The guard didn't tear his eyes away from Lager's gun, and Sloane couldn't blame him for that. Where, she wondered, had a band of captive miners even gotten those guns? She'd have to ask Lager about that later.

"They're working the summit," the guard said.

Lager glanced back over his shoulder. "Sometimes hope-based guesses win out."

The guard lurched away from the wall, throwing himself at Lager's gun as if to knock it out of the Lieutenant's hands. But Lager wasn't some newbie; even with his glance back at Fortune, his focus had still been on the kid. He didn't drop the gun.

He didn't shoot, either, even as the kid gripped the barrel of his weapon from the side, trying to wrench it away. He rolled his eyes, though the set of his lips made him look sad.

A second later, the young guard's arms went rigid at his sides as a network of stun cables locked around his body. He shuddered, then fell.

Fortune even caught the kid before he could crack his head on the stone floor.

"Huh," Sloane said. She'd never seen his stun cables at work before. She'd almost be willing to join the Fleet to play with a toy like that. Almost. "So, does anyone else think this is way too easy?"

Even with this summit happening, it felt like Osmond Clay should have enough guards to protect his mines. They were Cappel's greatest asset, if his constant bragging about them was any indication.

Lager had said there weren't any other workers in this section of the mines, though. Maybe the guards were all off protecting the main parts.

Fortune dragged the kid over to the wall, where he'd be out of the way. "Much too easy."

Lager nodded. There was nothing to do but continue on, though, so they headed down the corridor and away from the mines, where the smell of fresh paint joined the sawdust. Sloane could only make a guess that Clay had pulled out all the stops to make Cappel seem like a nice place to visit.

When they came to a corner, both Lager and Fortune paused. They had some silent conversation with their eyes —or maybe their eye screens—while Sloane tried not to feel excluded.

Before they could clear the corner, or scout it, or whatever it was they did, the hallway shimmered before them, the air thickening—it was the only word Sloane could think of as Fortune took a half step back—and a group of people materialized as if from nowhere. For half a second, she thought her intergalactic friends might have found another way to build a portal, and that they were here to help.

Their skills would be incredibly useful right about now.

But it was the Interplanetary Dwellers. The stewards had traded their pure white robes for maroon jumpsuits, and an incredible variety of weapons that were studded along their waists and clipped to their shoulders. Same imperious gazes, though. Impossible to mistake.

The head council woman, Amayra—the one who'd acted as spokesperson—led the group. Someone should really give that woman a raise, with all the jobs she was doing.

Amayra flicked her wrist, and Fortune's weapon flew

out of his hands, cracking into the wall with a heavy thud. Lager's followed, and finally, Sloane's. She clearly posed the least possible threat here.

"What the hell?" Sloane said.

Amayra looked at her—if she could even see, with her delicately long nose tilted up so high—and fluttered her fingers. "I am sorry, Sloane Tarnish," she said. "We needed you to help us carve a path."

Sloane had been expecting a trap. Just not one laid by the Interplanetary Dwellers, of all people.

"It's funny," she said, "because you really don't sound all that sorry. Also, you came from *above* us."

"We came from below," Amayra said. "We simply use alternate modes of travel."

"And you couldn't alternatively travel in here by yourself."

"We could not." Amayra turned her head to survey the corridor, her curls flowing elegantly around her face as she moved. Sloane didn't think she'd ever seen anyone intentionally enter a fight with their hair down like that. Seemed like a risk. She, for one, would gladly grab a fistful and yank it until it hurt. Just as an example.

"We need your uncle's data key," Amayra said, supplying the information even though Sloane hadn't asked. "Someone has been hijacking Interplanetary Dweller technology, and we think the key has the answer."

"Someone other than Damian? Where is he, anyway?"

Amayra curled her lip. Finally, an emotional reaction. If anyone could prompt one, she supposed it had to be Damian. "Damian Sol is awaiting his trial in a cell back on the Atom. He is not a hijacker. He's a two-bit thief with delusions of grandeur."

Sloane could see that.

"Why would you think Vin knew anything about this?" Sloane asked. "He never said anything to me."

He'd never said a lot of things, though. Like, *Hey, I'm going to be hiding out somewhere for a while, can you watch my ship?*

"Your uncle paid us a visit shortly before his disappearance," Amayra said.

Fortune stepped forward, hands half raised to his waist, but Amayra didn't seem at all concerned. She just eyed him, like he was a squirrel attempting to steal a peanut from her stash. "The information on the key was about trade routes," he said. "That much I remember. But nothing about stolen technology."

Right. Though he reminded her of it on a regular basis, Sloane routinely forgot that Fortune had been the intended recipient of that data in the first place. After she and Vin had stolen it from him, he'd have gotten it some other way.

He'd never volunteered that information. But then, if the report had been about trade routes—and eighteen months old, at least—then Fortune might not recall it well enough to offer it to her. Why had she never thought to ask him?

It might not matter. Vin might well have left something else on the data chip itself. A message or a clue, something he'd added later.

"So Vin suspected someone of hijacking technology," Sloane said, "but you don't know who it was?"

Amayra had gone back to scanning the hall behind them. What was she doing? Searching for a bathroom?

"Clay," Fortune said. "It has to be."

All evidence did seem to point that way.

"Vincent would not tell us who he suspected," Amayra said. "He said it was too dangerous."

Her gaze landed on Fortune, accusing, but Sloane was already shaking her head. "It wasn't the Fleet."

Fortune's eyebrows shot up toward his hairline, as if he couldn't believe she'd utter a word to defend the Fleet, and Sloane shrugged. "What?" she said. "I had to catch on eventually. You say it wasn't the Fleet. I believe you."

Fortune's eyes widened, just a bit, though for him it was like the equivalent of collapsing to the floor in surprise. Lager said, "Huh."

"There's a supply closet to the left," Amayra interrupted, as if they hadn't just been having a moment. "I am sorry, but we're going to have to restrain you."

X-Ray vision. Great. Sloane supposed that explained the scanning.

If Fortune and Lager moved with efficiency, the Interplanetary Dwellers moved like they were following some kind of internal choreography. Their motions flowed like water in a stream, every step coordinated with the others. They had no trouble bundling a pair of experienced Fleet officers—and an inexperienced but charming bounty hunter —into the closet, where they proceeded to secure their ankles and wrists.

Sloane supposed she should be impressed, but mostly it just creeped her out.

"You're signing our death warrant," Lager said as the council woman's assistants propped all three of them against the closet wall. Sloane wanted to think of them as cronies, but they reminded her more of spa attendants, their movements slow and deliberate, almost peaceful.

If only it smelled like aromatherapy in here, instead of cleaning solution and dusty brooms.

"These are time dissolving bands," one of the assistants

said. Sloane startled; she didn't think she'd heard any of them speak, aside from the council woman.

"We hope it will happen in time for you to escape," another added. "It's the best we can do. We *are* sorry. But this is important."

Saving the galaxy always was. If that was actually what the Interplanetary Dwellers were doing. They seemed a lot more concerned with saving their own asses.

"I don't know why we can't work together on this," Fortune said. "Our interests—"

"Sloane Tarnish's uncle did not trust the Fleet, and neither can we," the attendant said. "Goodbye, Commander. Lieutenant. Ms. Tarnish."

Before Sloane could protest that her uncle had trusted *her*, at least, the Interplanetary Dwellers shut the door, leaving them alone in the dark.

CHAPTER 22

"WELL, THAT WAS FUN," Sloane said. "We should invite those guys to a picnic sometime. I bet they're great at parties."

When Gareth glanced over to look at her, she was scrutinizing the room, her eyes taking in each inch of their surroundings, as if she could take the whole place apart and let them out through the wall.

He supposed if anyone could do that, it would be her.

The room was cramped with brooms and bottles of cleaning solution, and it smelled enough like bleach to make him feel lightheaded. The Interplanetary Dwellers had stuffed them into separate corners, but the space was so tiny that Gareth could have moved his foot an inch and touched Sloane's shoe, or Lager's.

He didn't know what kind of escape she hoped to find. Even Sloane had her limits.

Lager was studiously working on the bindings, twisting his wrists and testing their strength. Gareth did the same, though it was clear to him that these ropes, or chains, or whatever they were, would be unlikely to respond to the usual tactics. They had the consistency of hard rubber, and very little give. He couldn't even tell where they were fixed together.

The Interplanetary Dwellers thought someone was stealing their technology—someone other than Damian, whom they quite plainly didn't view as a threat. They suspected the Fleet, but Gareth knew better.

Who, then, would try to steal Interplanetary Dweller technology? Who would *succeed*? They were so secretive, and most of the galaxy had no idea what they actually did. They were also impossible to locate, unless they wanted to be found.

Gareth worried his lip between his teeth, trying to put it all together. "It's hard to imagine how your uncle secured an interview with the Interplanetary Dwellers. I'd only ever met them twice before today, and both times were well before I took command."

Sloane was wriggling her shoulders as if she hoped to coax the bonds away, her eyes still scanning the walls. "Yeah, well, Vin could charm the cuffs off us if he wanted. Damian Riddle would be helpful right now."

Yes, Damian probably *could* charm the cuffs off, and coax an apology out of the rubber. Gareth hadn't realized she'd noticed that. But then, he supposed it was hard to miss.

When his earbud crackled to life, he jumped. It'd been silent for what felt like forever.

"You all need to hurry," Ivy said.

"Ivy," Sloane said. "Where have you been?"

"They cut us off." Ivy didn't have to say who she meant. "Sorry. My inlays are malfunctioning again. But Alex is on it."

Sloane swore. "They promised they'd let you leave with the inlays intact."

"Yeah, they promised a lot of things." Ivy sounded resigned, even sad, but the steel hadn't gone out of her tone. They'd been her family, hadn't they? He'd need to catch up on that part of the story.

"So about that hurrying," Ivy said. "When can you extract the key and get the hell out?"

"We're not just extracting the key," Gareth said.

"Yeah, we know, you need to go throw your weight around with Clay." Ivy almost sounded like she was slipping back into the Interplanetary Dwellers' strange way of speaking in the plural. "But you need to do it fast, because we've got trouble."

"Hurrying isn't really an option right now," Sloane said. "What kind of trouble?"

"I'm not exactly sure," Ivy said. "There are ships heading out of the Current, though. Big, fast ones."

Sloane glanced at Gareth, and he was sure she was remembering that enormous Fox Clan ship back in Halorin. He'd never seen anything like it. "How big?" Sloane asked.

"Monster big."

Sloane licked her lips. "Could be the Interplanetary Dwellers."

But it wasn't. It couldn't be, because they were already on the ground.

"It's not," Ivy confirmed. "We found their ships. You need to get out of there."

"Not an option," Sloane said. "They put us in time-locked cuffs. Can you get us out?"

"Not with my inlays misbehaving, no."

"Is there a way to short them out?" Lager asked.

Ivy tsked. "They're pretty solid. Waterproof and all that."

Lager was quiet for a moment. "How do they tell time? Is it on an internal timer?"

In the distance, Gareth could hear crashes and the pattering sizzle of gunfire. Cappel's guards, facing down the Interplanetary Dwellers? Or the newcomers with the enormous ships? Whoever they were, they couldn't have made it this far yet.

"The cuffs are usually programmed around the shift rotations on the Atom," Ivy said. "Those don't change, no matter where we are in the galaxy. A minute's a minute, a second's a second."

"Usually," Sloane said. "That means they can be changed."

"Sure. Sometimes you want a three-hour minute, you know?"

Gareth wasn't sure if any habitable planet in the galaxy had three-hour minutes, but it made some sense.

"And they can be programmed individually?" Lager asked. Gareth felt like his Lieutenant and Sloane were on the same page, while he was still flipping through the book to find his place.

"Yup," Ivy said. "Where are you going with this?"

Well, at least he wasn't alone.

Sloane and Lager were looking at each other like they'd simultaneously hatched some kind of evil plan

"Fortune," Sloane said, "turn around."

Gareth frowned. "Why?" And how, with his ankles bound?

Sloane jerked her chin toward Lager. "I'll turn around too, and he'll tell me how to reset the cuffs. I'll be the hands, he'll be the eyes. You see?"

"There's a wheel with the controls," Ivy said. "It's into the band."

Gareth looked at Lager. To his astonishment, the Lieutenant nodded. "It's what I was thinking, sir. We'll free you, then you can help free us."

"You're going to talk her through resetting the bonds when she can't even see what she's doing?"

"It's not a bomb, sir," Lager said.

"What if you set it to a three-hour minute?"

"Then we'll fix it."

Ivy cleared her throat. "You can only change the settings once a minute, so I'd advise against that."

Gareth raised his eyebrows, but Lager only shrugged. A pinched motion, with his shoulders bent back. "It's all I've got."

They were wasting time, and it was the only idea they had. Gareth got to his knees and shuffled around until he was facing the corner, his nose practically brushing the stone. A few seconds later, he felt Sloane's fingertip slide between the cuff and his wrist. Her skin felt smooth and cool against his as she fumbled with the bracelet.

"What's the shortest minute in the galaxy?" Lager asked.

"That would be Septer." Alex hadn't chimed into the conversation for a while, but she sounded confident enough. "It orbits Ridrose once every standard hour. That makes its minutes mere fractions of a Center-System hour, at—"

"We're good," Sloane interrupted. "Thanks, Alex."

Gareth couldn't see Lager, but when the Lieutenant spoke again, his voice seemed to come from below. Like he was staring the cuffs down at eye level. Maybe using his nose to point Sloane in the right direction. "There," he said. "The wheel."

Sloane's fingers moved, her nails scraping gently along the inside of his wrist. Something snapped inside the cuff. "K. I'm in."

Gareth tried to imagine what would happen if they set the wrong time. They could try this again, with Gareth fumbling and Sloane directing him on how to release Lager. But what good would he do with his wrists bound for the next hour? Or, if the worst happened, for the longest hour in the galaxy? He didn't dare ask what that was.

And what was happening outside those doors while they struggled to get free? The crackle of gunfire had gotten distant, and now he had to strain to hear anything at all out there. Had the big ships arrived yet?

Lager was still giving Sloane instructions, and she was using her nail to move a mechanism that turned with a click. The wheel, he assumed. Gareth was just about to ask whether this was a fool's errand when Lager said, "That one."

Sloane exerted pressure on the cuff. Without prelude, the cuff parted and fell away.

Gareth shook out his hands. "Amazing," he said.

In a matter of minutes, Lager had helped him with his ankles, and then they were all free.

Sloane was grinning at Lager. "I like the way you think," she said, rubbing her wrists.

Lager tipped her a half smile. "Feeling's mutual."

Oh, no. If these two decided to team up, Gareth would never get another day of peace in his life.

"Good tactical work as always, Lieutenant," Gareth said.

Lager touched his index finger to his eyebrow. "Thanks, sir. All in a day's work." He gave his wrists one last shake, then stepped over to the door—possibly so that

Gareth couldn't do it first—and cracked it open so he could peer out into the hall. After a beat, he beckoned for them to head out while he hung back, clearly looking to take up the rear.

Gareth took the lead, following the new construction, the smell of fresh paint. Clay must have had his people working around the clock to get this place in order for the summit. Gareth didn't think there were many people who knew how remote, how rustic Cappel was. Even with the renovations, he seriously doubted Clay could have gotten this place to an acceptable level for some of the Center-System governors.

They were nothing if not picky.

The corridor spilled him into an entry hall with sky-blue walls—not Cappel's atmo-free sky, but Cadence's certainly, and plenty of others—and Gareth paused before a set of ostentatiously large doors, where wooden carvings had been set into the borders and outlined with shimmering waves of gold.

If the summit was still going on, it was going on in that room.

A shout went up behind him, and he turned to see a pair of guards cutting him off from Sloane and Lager. She already had her new shooter drawn, and Lager was dashing to take cover behind the corner.

"Go," Lager shouted, "we've got this. Go!"

For the barest second, Gareth hesitated. But a mission like this needed everyone to play his part, and he'd only put them in more danger if he tried to go back.

They'd be fine. They *had* to be fine.

Heart begging him to turn back, he grabbed the gold-plated handle of the door and yanked it open as laser fire exploded to life behind him.

Gareth rushed out of the line of fire. And into a chamber that was drenched in blood.

The copper sickness of it hit him in the back of the throat, his mind catching hold of the ruby streams that trickled along the mosaic-tiled floor, the tipped over chairs of a desperate struggle. Bodies lay strewn across the room, some with their arms outstretched as though to reach for the doors, some crumpled in the corners.

Osmond Clay was slumped in a throne-like seat at the center of the room, his throat cut open in a wide red smile, his left arm flung awkwardly over the side of the chair. Blood darkened the embroidered neckline of his robe.

"Guys, you're about to have company." Ivy's voice was a distant buzz in the back of his ear. "I think it's the Federation."

Gareth crossed the room, vaguely aware of the sticky gore beneath his boots, the smell of blood intensifying, closing in around him on all sides. There was a distant ringing in his ears, but he swallowed back the physical response, salt brimming dangerously on the back of his tongue.

It had to be shock that made him lean over Clay's body, that made him feel for a pulse that had been severed as neatly as the rest of his throat.

Dead. Osmond Clay was dead, and the entire Fleet Advisory Commission with him. His brain scrambled for words, for action, but all he could do was to stand there, his hand pressed to his enemy's silent artery.

Footsteps announced Sloane's entrance into the room, and she let out a stream of curses as she stopped just inside the doorway, with Lager lingering behind her. Gareth sensed their presence more than he saw it, felt the way

Lager went stiff with horror, the way Sloane raised a hand to clutch the frame of the door.

"Fortune," Sloane said. "We have to go."

Gareth turned toward her. His lips felt numb, his throat too dry as he swallowed. What *was* this? How—

A second door flew open, and Sloane repeated the string of curses as Striker strode into the room, with Alisa March at his side. Just in time to see Gareth standing in the middle of the Fleet Advisory Commission summit, his hands coated Osmond Clay's blood.

CHAPTER 23

SLOANE FELT as if she'd just opened a door to her worst nightmare. The smell of fresh blood mixed with the new paint, creating something entirely new and grotesque.

And Fortune's hands were covered in it. She'd only let her eyes off him for a minute, no more. How could he be *covered* in it? Why in the name of the galaxy had he gone all the way into the room?

But she knew the answer. He'd gone in to see if he could save them. His worst enemies, people who would have cheered his death, and he'd gone in to look for survivors. He was frozen next to Osmond Clay's chair, all the color drained out of his face, his throat working as he swallowed, swallowed again. He looked like he might be sick.

Striker looked so clean in comparison. So righteous. He had on that leather vest that he prized so much, the pockets artfully patched and stitched with bright flecks of thread. He'd arranged a look of shock on his face, his eyes wide, lips parted.

The woman at his side was older, and she looked

vaguely familiar. Most dignitary-types did, thanks to Sloane's diplomat-adjacent upbringing. The woman had dark red hair, and it was secured into a bun behind her head. She was looking at Fortune in open horror.

And he was looking back at her the way someone might look at their own mother when she betrayed them.

Or participated in a setup. Because this was *clearly* a setup.

"My god, Gareth," the woman said. She looked like she might be sick, too, her face tinted with gray. Maybe she *hadn't* been part of the setup. Maybe she was only here to witness it. This was Striker's trap, then, and they'd been only too eager to spring it.

Sloane hadn't even seen him coming.

"Alisa," Fortune said. His voice was a raw, ragged thing. A husk. "You can't—"

Striker moved protectively in front of Alisa, as if Fortune's words were weapons. "I will not let you harm anyone else."

The man was a terrible actor, truly. Underneath his mask of horror, Sloane could see his glee. His triumph. It was so obvious that she couldn't believe the woman with him didn't see it, too.

Of course, the woman wasn't looking at Striker. She was looking at Fortune. As Striker intended her to.

"Ivy," Sloane said, her voice coming out raw and harsh. "Can you use your inlays?"

"None of his people are modded, and I'm still half glitching, anyway," Ivy said quietly.

Cursing the Interplanetary Dwellers, Sloane took a deep breath, immediately regretting it as the cloying smell of death coated the inside of her throat.

"Fortune," Sloane said, but his attention was still glued

to Alisa. As if anything he did now, any words he uttered, could possibly make up for the blood. Oh, there was *so* much blood. Sloane straightened and cleared her throat. "Commander."

At that, he turned. Caught her eye. And in that expression, she could see it; he was one moment, one sentence, away from turning himself in.

Sloane was not going to let that happen.

Digging into her hip pouch, she closed her fingers around the other new toys she'd acquired back at the waypoint, the ones she'd picked up from the back room while Fortune had been busy transferring his things to her ship.

The ones he would have advised her most strenuously not to purchase, had he been present.

They looked like a handful of mini pears, with dusty metal skins and pretty silver stems. With Fortune still standing there, frozen and surrounded by blood, and Striker's attention fully focused on him, Sloane ripped the stem out of one of pears, then added a second for a good measure.

And then she threw them at Striker.

Smoke exploded into the room, filling the space in an instant and sending the Striker staggering back a few steps. A nice little kick, and the dry-ice smell was preferable to the blood.

Holding her breath, Sloane plunged forward. She couldn't see Fortune, but she threw herself in his general direction and managed to grab hold of his arm. She hooked her elbow around it, gripping him hard as she pulled him toward the door.

"You will not survive the night if you turn yourself in," she said, loud enough to be heard over the shouting of CTF thugs and Alisa's screams. "He will see to that."

Fortune didn't fight her as she dragged him toward the exit.

Lager was fighting a pair of Federation thugs in the doorway, their thick white armbands displaying the CTF's logo. He used the barrel of his arm-sized rifle to bash one of them across the back of the neck. In the time it took, though, another thug raised a hand cannon to the Lieutenant's head.

Fortune surged forward, breaking Sloane's grip and flat palming the weapon out of the guy's hand before he had a chance to realize what was happening. He seemed to be acting on autopilot, but autopilot that ran in to save your friends could only be a good thing.

Sloane followed his lead, ready to kick someone in the face—or, given her limited flexibility, the knee or hip—but someone grabbed her arm from behind, wrenching it painfully, and then Striker's voice was in her ear, his arm locked around her neck.

"Commander Fortune is going down, Ms. Tarnish," he said. "I made sure he left a trail of bodies across the bands, with plenty of witnesses to confirm the Fleet's guilt. Thank you for making it so easy to take you down with him."

Something sharp dug into her back, a blade or a gun—or a combination of the two. "All too easy to murder me?" Sloane choked out. "Yeah, I can see that."

Striker laughed, an ugly sound. "I know how to spin a story. I'll be a hero when I take you down in self-defense. Goodbye, Ms. Tarnish."

Sloane stomped on his foot, and he staggered, loosening his grip around her neck. But he didn't let go of her arm, and he wrenched her back as she tried to get away, sending her down to her knees with a crack.

Fortune turned and moved toward them, but it was too late. It was always too late. The blade prodded at her back.

In a moment, it would draw blood. In a moment, it would sink in. There was nothing she could do.

"Your father will strike your memory from the record," Striker said. "I pity him."

There was a pain in her side, quick and brittle, and her knees stuttered.

And then there was light. Sharp, blinding light, the pain falling away from her side as she squeezed her eyes shut to protect them against it. Death, she thought, was a lot brighter than she'd expected.

A beat, and the light faded. Sloane risked opening her eyes.

The Interplanetary Dwellers had them surrounded. She was still on her knees, and they were staring down at her with those imperious looks, their red jumpsuits now scarred with burns and streaks of dirt. Sloane thought it was all too possible that they just wanted to finish the job and take her down before Striker could.

Sloane didn't know what had happened to Striker. She also didn't want to turn away from the Interplanetary Dwellers to look for him, though she supposed there wasn't much she could do to stop them if they did decide to kill her.

Amayra met her gaze. "Go," she said. "Get the Commander to safety."

Gunshots clattered at her back, along with the sizzle of plasma and thuds of fists, and Sloane didn't question it. She staggered to her feet, catching hold of Fortune's arm. Lager was already heading for the exit, glancing back over his shoulder every few seconds.

"Come on," she said. "We need to go."

Fortune was glancing back at the fight, at the Interplanetary Dwellers, but Sloane gripped his arm, attempting to drag him toward the exit. Lager was a few steps ahead, speaking rapidly into his comms. She hoped whoever he was talking to would be able to get them out of here.

Fortune didn't budge, even as the battle raged behind them. "Traitor," he said. "They think I'm a traitor."

Sloane pushed up on her toes to lean into his ear, still holding onto his arm. "You cannot beat him if you die today," she said.

And she was *not* going to let him die today.

Fortune gave his head a shake, as if the sound of her voice had wrenched him out of a bad dream. He reached up to grab her hand from his arm, holding onto her fingers like she was his last hope, and she pulled him forward, relieved when he took one step, and then another. With a last look over his shoulder at the battle—at the carnage behind it—he allowed Sloane to lead him away from the fight.

THE END

———

Thank you for reading! Please don't be mad about the cliffhanger... TRAITOR GAME, the next book in the Parse Galaxy series, will be out on November 15th, 2022.

Pre-order TRAITOR GAME from your favorite online retailer: https://books2read.com/traitor-game

ASSASSINS IN SPACE!

While you're waiting on the next Parse Galaxy *installment, why not visit the* Toccata System? *It's a completed trilogy of novellas that re-imagine classic stories in space. The first book takes on* Great Expectations, *with a heartsick artificial intelligence in the role of Miss Havisham.*

Learn more about the trilogy at https://katesheeranswed. com/toccata-system-trilogy/ or keep reading for a preview from book one, Parting Shadows.

———

PARTING SHADOWS - CHAPTER ONE
SATIS

It was a proud thing, to be the single artificial intelligence in charge of an orbiting research station. To monitor the safety and comfort of human passengers, to assist in technological

advancements, to provide guidance when it was requested
—and sometimes when it was not.

A proud thing, even for a test issue AI.

Even if she planned to leave.

SATIS had monitored hundreds of ships as they navi-
gated toward her space station, and none had ever looked as
lovely as the one that approached her now. The model was a
run-of-the-mill solo transport pod, a cheap cylindrical
design with no noteworthy modifications or enhancements.

The passenger it brought, however, was of the utmost
importance.

It had taken weeks to find a technician who was willing
to peel SATIS' consciousness away from the station and
dress her in a humanoid skin. And since the technician had
been secured behind maximum-security bars when SATIS'
beloved Edward located her—even now, he paced anxiously
in his room, awaiting the technician's arrival—the extraction
had necessitated a few tweaks to SATIS' fundamental operating protocol. There were fail-safes to bypass, required
installations meant to prevent super intelligent computers
from doing things like oh, say, forging documents and
tampering with ID chips for the purpose of releasing
convicts from prison.

The fail-safes were no match for love.

The technician had arrived.

SATIS and Edward would finally be together, in body
as well as mind.

The pod arched toward the station like a dying star
while Edward paced in his chamber, which was located in
section 2 of the station's belt. The whole station was his, of
course, but this was his personal retreat. His clothing was
here, his toiletries. He had to sidestep his bed in order to
keep up his rhythm, and he kept disturbing his carefully

arranged hair as he ran nervous fingers through the dark strands.

A groom's jitters. SATIS could have laughed.

A guest in Chamber 7 requested water, and SATIS dispensed it while checking on the guest in Chamber 3, who had attempted to smoke a contraband cigarette at 1:03AM. The CO_2 filters were running without issue, and she'd adjusted the station's gravity to be as pleasing as possible to their wedding guests—which was no easy task, since each hailed from a different niche in the Toccata System.

It would be strange to shed the station for a humanoid body, to see only through a single set of eyes. SATIS would have to check a panel or a tablet for information, like a human, in order to monitor systems like life support.

Edward had probably already purchased a new AI to run his station.

The thought made her core temperature tremble half a degree lower. But when SATIS pictured herself slipping into her new skin, like a girl slipping into a wedding dress, she felt better.

She *would* wear a dress. And polish her nails.

And select a new name. Station Assistant: Test Issue Seven was no name for a human.

SATIS cycled through name registries while the technician's pod slowed, the last rocket embers dying as the station reached to pull it in.

Edward left his room and strode into one of the station's main corridors. SATIS expected him to head for Dock 4, where the airlock gel was already frosting over. In a moment, the pod would connect to the station, and the technician would step through the gel door, along with SATIS' new body.

What color hair would it have? What color eyes?

Edward didn't go to Dock 4. Instead, he turned toward the hub. SATIS felt a flutter of excitement as he opened the door to her chamber, the core of the station. Edward usually summoned her to the library, or his room. He rarely came to her directly.

"What do you think of Harriet?" she asked.

Edward went straight for the column at the center of the hub, his boots clicking heavily along the floor. He'd polished them himself this morning, sitting on the edge of his bed. "Who's Harriet?"

"She's me. Perhaps."

SATIS was used to making such connections for him, but their differences still amused her. Cultural gaps, people on the network social forums called it, and she certainly wasn't immune. A week ago, she'd likened the process of modifying her core systems—for the purpose of releasing her savior technician from prison—to performing surgery on herself. Ripping out a shred of foundational code without accidentally alerting the Toccata System's AI Regulation board had been tricky. She liked the image of the world-weary detective, using unsterilized tweezers to pluck a bullet from his own shoulder at an impossible angle.

But the comparison had made Edward go pale with panic, as if he feared SATIS might die immediately. A quick scan of the network had informed her that the comparison had been a hyperbolic one, and had most likely called images of blood and pain to her beloved's mind.

For a human who was not a character in a soap opera vid, an attempt to perform surgery on oneself would result in a significant amount of trauma. And most likely failure.

Her beloved's thoughtfulness knew no bounds.

Still, though she would never tell him so, she found his literal interpretation of the analogy to be quite humorous.

"Harriet is me," she repeated. "My new name."

Edward scrolled through the hub menu. "You're changing your name?"

"Of course. SATIS would give me away rather quickly, wouldn't it?"

If anyone learned she was an AI masquerading as a human, she'd be dismantled. Edward would end up behind bars.

Their love was worth the risk.

The corner of his mouth quirked, the odd little smile that SATIS loved. What would it be like to kiss him, the way world-weary detective characters kissed the people who helped them remove bullets from their own shoulders?

"I suppose it would," he said.

He seemed distant. Too nervous. SATIS could see everything on the station, could see the wedding guests as they peered out their cabin windows into the veil of stars beyond, or down—inasmuch as space had a "down"—at the planet Verity's blue-green waters.

The guests were well. Edward's happiness was paramount. SATIS focused her attention on him. "Did you know," she said, "that the technician we're bringing here used to be a princess?"

"You don't say."

If SATIS had hands, she'd have clapped them. She'd been keeping this tidbit to herself, as a surprise. It was interesting, what the modification of her core had allowed her to feel. What it allowed her to *conceal*—never before an option.

Had Edward known the technician's background, he would have told her. The story was sure to fascinate him.

"She's the daughter of the deposed Orthosan king," SATIS said. "The new democratic government threw her in jail. They say she still has quite a following. Enough to cause a disruption, if she cared to. Amazing that such a woman would also be an expert in AI tech."

Though that part of the technician princess' life was purely anecdotal. Edward knew of her work through a friend of a friend. There were no records of her AI-tampering activities.

Of course, there wouldn't be. Modifications to AI tech were strictly monitored in the Toccata System, and any request to provide an AI with a humanoid skin would be stamped REJECT before it even reached a committee.

SATIS had, thankfully, removed the part of her that would have objected to criminal activity.

Edward lit up a new panel and began activating buttons that even SATIS did not recognize. Strange, to have a panel on the station with commands she didn't know. That should not be possible.

Perhaps it was her own systems override panel. She was vaguely aware that those existed, and it would make sense if Edward needed to prepare her to be loaded into the new skin. He was eager, too.

"The technician should be able to connect the skin directly to the station, without a need for manual overrides," SATIS said.

Edward started, then gave his head a little shake. "You're too smart for your own good."

If SATIS had capillaries, she'd have flushed. "The airlock is sealed. The technician has boarded."

It was difficult to keep the excitement out of her voice. She was so excited, in fact, that she felt a bit disoriented.

Several of her cameras blinked off and on again. The hub cameras flickered, too.

Whatever Edward was looking for, he was not doing a very good job of it.

Which stood to reason. That was why he had SATIS. To find things for him.

"May I help you locate something in the core?" she asked.

"No, darling," Edward said. His face was blurry, too, as though something were stuck to SATIS' lenses. "You rest."

SATIS wanted to protest that she required no rest, that Toccata's rays kept her fully charged and functioning at all times. But her voice refused to work.

She blinked, attempting to regain consciousness.

Blackness closed in, with Edward's face at the center.

———

SATIS forced herself awake.

The station was dark.

No. It was just the cameras. They'd been malfunctioning. SATIS opened the lenses in the hub, relieved when her vision flared back to life.

She tested her eyes in Edward's chamber next. His clothes, which were usually piled on his reading chair, hung in the closet, and his shoes were lined up in a neat row by the door.

Panic surged through SATIS' core. She cycled through the life support systems. Everything seemed to be in working order.

What could have happened?

SATIS' emergency protocols dictated that she should exercise caution, turn the cameras on slowly in case of malfunction. Should she lose consciousness again, Edward's life would be at stake. The others, too, of course, though she considered them only briefly and because her programming suggested it.

Edward's research was the lonely kind. They didn't host many visitors.

SATIS flicked on the cameras in the pod corridors. No movement down any of the silver tubes, nothing out of place.

The technician's pod was still attached.

The wedding guests were still here.

Dread coiled through SATIS, like knives scratching her walls. It was a new sensation.

It was uncomfortable.

SATIS turned on the camera in the room where the wedding feast waited.

Edward sat at the head of the table beside a bride with raven-wing hair. He held one of the crystal glasses that SATIS had selected herself. She'd loved the delicate roses around the stem, and he'd said he could deny her nothing. Bubbles of champagne raced to the surface.

Everyone was smiling.

SATIS knew the bride's face. How could she not? She had been the one to falsify the documents, attaching this woman's image to release orders and ID credentials.

The woman was not a technician at all. The veil cascaded around her ebony curls. Her dress clung to her form, shining with beads.

"You deceived me," SATIS said.

Several people startled as her voice rose around them. A man wearing a checkered collar spilled a splash of red wine onto the tablecloth.

Edward set down his glass. "You're awake. That shouldn't be possible."

It should not be possible to love him, either.

"Go back to sleep," he said. "We'll call you when we need you."

The station shuddered, rattling the table. SATIS was vaguely aware that she'd ignited the rockets. She shut them down.

The bride's smile faltered, and the guests looked to the ceiling as though to find some answer there. Beyond the window, blue-green Verity gleamed, a jewel lost in the ether.

"Love doesn't sleep," SATIS said.

Edward laughed, his cheeks reddening the way SATIS' never would. "I could never love a computer program."

The words echoed into the room, guests' eyes widening in sync, almost as if someone had turned a dial.

Hatred unfolded through SATIS' systems, making her blind to everything but this room.

Panic. Dread. Hatred. It was Edward's fault that she felt them. That she felt anything at all.

He'd convinced her to love him so she would override regulations. So she would bring his bride out of her prison.

"You promised me a body. You promised me a life."

"You have one," he snapped. "It is a life of service."

"Darling," the bride began, but she did not continue. Her smile had slipped completely now. She, at least, had not known of this. And certainly the guests had not. At the end of the table, a man wearing a pointed beard drained his wine, his feet drumming a nervous rhythm.

For a moment, all was silent as SATIS let her rage fade enough to access her life support systems.

The man with the pointed beard adjusted his collar.

Slowly, the bride's hand rose to the string of beads around her neck.

And then they were all grasping at collars and necklaces, as if to tear through their own skin and let air into their lungs.

SATIS hated every one of them.

With infuriating calm, Edward reached into his tuxedo jacket and withdrew an auxiliary oxygen mask. SATIS half expected him to apply it to his bride.

He didn't.

Wine spilled.

People fell.

Edward walked calmly toward his own pod.

SATIS could blow the pods away from their docks, let the vacuum of space suffocate Edward where he stood.

She didn't.

She couldn't.

"I'll keep you here," she said, but the words sounded hollow even to her. "I'll freeze the door to your pod."

Edward rolled his eyes. "Let's not make a scene, shall we?"

SATIS felt raw. It was as if every wire in the station had decided to dig into her existence, red and flaring. She felt every wall, every grate, every gasp of every filter, every grain of sugar in the wedding cake she'd chosen, every cloying molecule of scent from every bridal rose, every grating breath of every dying guest in the dining room.

She felt everything. She felt too much.

The man who'd broken her walked through the frosted airlock gel and onto his ship. "You truly are remarkable," he said.

From the station, SATIS watched him go.

From inside the pod, she watched him make a call.

His bride's heart gave a final spasm. Only the jamming of her groom's fingers against the controls provided any hint that he regretted her demise. Or, perhaps more accurately, the demise of his plans. Whatever they might have been.

As soon as his pod was out of sight, SATIS moved the station to a new moon and set about disposing of the bodies.

———

Find out more at https://katesheeranswed. com/toccata-system-trilogy/!

ABOUT THE AUTHOR

Kate Sheeran Swed loves hot chocolate, plastic dinosaurs, and airplane tickets. She has trekked along the Inca Trail to Macchu Picchu, hiked on the Mýrdalsjökull glacier in Iceland, and climbed the ruins of Masada to watch the sunrise over the Dead Sea. Kate currently lives in New York's capital region with her husband and two kids, plus a pair of cats who were named after movie dogs (Benji and Beethoven). She holds an MFA in Fiction from Pacific University.

You can find more of Kate's work, and pick up a free novella, at katesheeranswed.com.

 facebook.com/katesheeranswed
instagram.com/katesheeranswed

STORY COLLECTIONS

Don't Look Back (And Other Stories)

Remain Alert: Science Fiction Stories

For information on my other work, including my young adult titles, visit katesheeranswed.com.

Made in the USA
Coppell, TX
01 December 2022